Herbert Martin

Britomart

A novel

Herbert Martin

Britomart
A novel

ISBN/EAN: 9783337050948

Printed in Europe, USA, Canada, Australia, Japan

Cover: Foto ©Andreas Hilbeck / pixelio.de

More available books at **www.hansebooks.com**

Britomart.

A Novel.

BY

Mrs. Herbert Martin,

Author of

" Bonnie Lesley," " Common Clay,"
" A Man and a Brother," etc.

.

" Faire Britomart, whose constant mind
Ne reckt of ladies love . . .
She forward went
With stedfast courage and stout hardiment.
Ne evil thing she feared, ne evil thing she ment."

In Three Volumes.

Vol. I.

London:

Richard Bentley & Son,

Publishers in Ordinary to Her Majesty the Queen.

1893.

BRITOMART.

CHAPTER I.

A SOMBRE looking room, the walls well lined with grave-hued books, a grey twilight stealing in, damp and cheerless, nothing within to enliven the aspect of the heavy, handsome, yet unhomelike interior of Mr. Trevenna's library, but the red sparkle of a fire. The only occupant of the room, a pale, grey, thin, elderly man, lying rather than sitting in a lounging chair, who, having ceased reading from inability to see any longer, was doing nothing now but staring gloomily enough on this same fire

The large old house was silent as a tomb, the servants were out of hearing, stillness brooded like a presence, the fall of a cinder now and then sounded startlingly loud. The firelight faintly illumined the stern yellow-white face of Richard Trevenna, and lurked in the iron-grey of his locks, thinning on the bony temples, but pretty long and thick below. The deeply sunken eyes were those of a man weary of life, and one who was more used to bitterness and hate, than the kindly affections of humanity. It was an intellectual face enough, but dissatisfied, restless, and profoundly ill at ease, physical suffering and decay having been busy at the work of sharpening and lining the face, which an unsatisfied. soul had begun. And now whatever of good or evil, of disappointment, desire, failure, discontent had been, everything, except the dreary pause of stagnation when the end is near, was over. Mr. Trevenna lived on, looking for nothing, hoping for nothing, with few motives in life, with even a want of energy in despising. Life had been a failure, it was nearly over, and nothing more mattered much. Yet one or two sensations survived, some pains still faintly gnawed, something of evil and of good still lingered in the weary world-worn heart. Both the evil and the good had often surprised the man himself; his own life, his own character had always been a struggle and a contradiction; he only knew that what he had meant had never been accomplished, and what he had accomplished had often done ill; and now it was a late hour even for regrets. What did anything signify? Was he not a spark, to glow for an instant, then extinguished for ever? But a spark's brief moment may set up a conflagration. Sometimes he writhed under the burdens of his memory, and the impotent misery of every outlook; at others some better longing, some nobler desire rose and struggled for a last expression ere everything was closed, and Richard Trevenna's page of life was turned for ever. He moved his long, thin body restlessly, and uttered a sort of groan. He was waiting in the shades already till the boat of Charon touched his desolate shore.

A clanging ring at the front-door bell echoed suddenly through the silent house, and made him quiver with a nervous start. He never had but three visitors, his doctor, his lawyer, and his old college friend Grey—it could be but one of these. Probably Grey. Yes. The door opened to admit the little, stooping, hesitating figure of the one man on earth that he might call his friend. The sight of the Master of —— College was the only vision of the long dull day that roused any sense of satisfaction in Mr. Trevenna's heart. They had always been as different as men can be ever since the old days, thirty odd years ago when they were chums at College, and when young Dick Trevenna was a reckless, brilliant, hot-tempered, thin-skinned, yet lovable scape-grace, and his friend Edmund Grey the quietest, shyest, steadiest young plodder, with grand ideas and an enthusiasm which made food for cynical laughter, but which had outlived a thousand heart-beats of the fierce, transient emotions of his friend. Grey had not so much changed as fossilized. Trevenna was utterly re-made from those times of their youth. Yet the pure-minded, gentle, ascetic, religious old scholar, who still believed, still loved, and still laboured on in a blind, persistent, often blundering fashion, a thousand times deceived yet still inclined to trust, could never get out of the habit of friendship for the man over whose life he had mourned in his quiet way, ever since the early parting of the ways when

Trevenna's path went hopelessly awry. Both were now old bachelors, apparently on the same footing, into both lives the influence of women had come and departed, in one case only to spoil and to sear, in the other to leave a faint sad echo of what might have been a lovely harmony. Once, and only once, the shy maiden soul of Edmund Grey had opened to passion. He never made up his mind or had the courage to confess it—it was always to be, and never was. Some one stepped in with the confident boldness of a different nature and picked his rose; no other ever seemed worth plucking since that had faded away untouched by him ages ago. Since then he had grown quietly old in his solitude, with a lock and key on his silent heart; but he was still young in mind. He still believed in good women, and liked to watch the romances of other people from behind the monastery grille of his own secluded life.

A shy, stammering, modest man, with no power of expansion or expression, doing kind things by stealth as if they were sins; awkward, plain, grey, yet with a certain silent beauty in the serene benediction of his gentle look. Few people knew him, but not a few dearly liked the courteous, considerate, reserved old bachelor who hated to give pain, but bore it himself with the calmest stoicism. A scholar, a Christian, and a gentleman, yet with a sort of sympathy for ignorance, for doubt, and for sin, sprung from the compassion of a gentle heart. He never knew how to find fault, some people said he was a great deal too lax to have such a post as he held at the University, close to which Mr. Trevenna's property was situated, and where Mr. Grey had lived for five-and-thirty years.

The little timid figure came sidling in, and the old friends took hands; both had undemonstrative manners, and only just touched each other for a moment as coldly if they were as mere acquaintances.

" I can't get up," Mr. Trevenna said, in a low-pitched, harsh voice—harsh, but not loud. " I am rather extra bad to-day, with what Brett calls neuralgic pains. Sit down, and stir that sleepy fire. It's an accursed day."

" No, no," Mr. Grey said deprecatingly, as if even the weather needed a defender, "not so bad. Chilly—we expect chilly weather in April, but with a feeling of spring. You get cold from want of exercise." He tried feebly to stir the fire into a blaze ; but his hands were awkward in wielding any weapon but a pen, he nearly put out the flame instead of enlivening it, and dropped the poker with a clatter which made his friend start and swear between his teeth.

It always hurt Mr. Grey to hear Trevenna swear, though he was used to it, and he hurried into nervous apologies, as trying to quiet things, he made more noise than before.

" Oh, damn it, Grey, leave the fire-irons alone. Be content with having put out my poor fire, and tortured my nerves. Sit still, if you can, and don't attempt to do anything with those useless hands of yours. Let's hear if you have any news ; yet, don't tell it me, on second thoughts, for I am incapable of feeling any interest in anybody but myself, and it's not worth while pretending to do so. The only possible thing that will do me any good at this moment, is to growl about my own sensations—yet that's stupid enough, and the relief is transient."

" You are feeling bad ? " the little man asked, anxiously, clasping his hands, and squeezing them between his knees, one of his tricks of action. He peered, with his soft, short-sighted eyes, into the worn, haggard, yellow face of his friend.

" Bad ? Well, that's a mild word !

Grey, I'm feeling all the pains of body and all the weariness of spirit of which this vile essence of ours is capable, I believe. I suppose it's all right, I should —for virtuous people would find some virtuous reason for it, I've no doubt. But I never asked to be born. I might have been consulted."

"What does—what does Brett say?" There was a sort of stammer in Mr. Grey's speech, which was never fluent or facile, and in emotion almost all power of expression seemed to fail him. He never could put into words the compassionate tenderness of his soul.

"Brett? Oh, he talks cheerful lies, after the manner of his kind, till I drive him into a corner, when he admits, what I know already, that few and evil are the days that remain to me. I shouldn't mind if every one of them didn't last a year, and every night stretch into six. It's all infinite tedium ; perhaps, when the pain is sharpest, it is not the most difficult to get on. Eh! But this is delightful chat to entertain a friend with! Suppose we talk politics, religion, or scandal. You start a subject, old man, and I'll do my best to chime in."

" Is Geoffrey coming down? I thought you expected him?"

The question brought a frown on the already lowering forehead, and a sneer on Mr. Trevenna's grim mouth.

"Oh, Mr. Geoff finds metal more attractive. He doesn't care to come down here to be bored by an infernally sour old uncle. He's philandering after the daughter of that most abominable parvenu, James Field, from what I hear — for, though I'm laid on the shelf, I manage to get information, you see—a pretty, silly, frivolous, flirting thing. I'd rather he married any one else, almost. I detest that fellow Field."

" Do you know him?"

"Yes; at least I have known him, and known things of him, quite enough to loathe him, and that loud, vulgar, fool of a wife of his. But I ought to expect little better of Geoffrey; he has done nothing for years past but disappoint me." After a pause he went on, with fierce suddenness, jerking out his words as if they were difficult to force from his lips. "I've been thinking over things—I've plenty of time to think — I'm nearly resolved to make an entire change in the disposition of my property—I have other reasons besides being disgusted with Geoffrey."

Mr. Grey murmured some vague, inarticulate reply, moving first one foot then another, with aimless spasmodic motions. All that was audible seemed to deprecate the blame on Mr. Trevenna's nephew. The other answered his spirit, rather than his word.

"Oh yes; I dare say Geoffrey's no

worse, no more selfish, dissipated, heartless, or foolish than other young men.
They are bad, as a rule. I tell you
it isn't only that I'm displeased with
him. You remember that talk we had
a month ago, when I was taken worse,
and you thought I was dying?"

Mr. Grey murmured a faint assent.

"You spoke up strongly for once, old
man. Upon my life you surprised me!
When a quiet, shy fellow, like you, fires
up and has his say, I suppose one is
naturally impressed. You know what
you told me you thought of the past—
what your idea was of the future?"

"Yes, I know; I—I think so still,
Trevenna."

"Of course you do. Quiet as you seem
you are as obstinate in your notions as a
mule. Well, I suppose you stirred up a
sort of half dormant feeling in me. Call
it a remorse if you will. As you put it—
—if there's anything in your ideas—there

does seem a claim, a wrong. I put inquiries on foot. Of course my lawyer knows where they are, they are regularly paid, and all that ; but personally I knew very little. I did not care to inquire or to hear. I have nearly made up my mind to do what you are so keen on, Grey. But it's late in the day. I don't think it will do my soul—if I have a soul—or any one else's much good. But perhaps it may be right. One leaves that sort of question to you experts. Just as I allow Brett to talk learnedly about my inside, to diagnose and to experimentalize in his own depart- ment, so I consider *you*, old man, a scientist in moral questions. If you are right or wrong, at any rate you've been consistent, and you've given your life to it. You have no doubts on moral questions, you hesitate an hour as to the choice of a hat, and you grope about in difficult bits of knowledge between this belief and that, but you speak like an oracle where conscience is concerned, and are as confident as if you had received an inspiration from the supernatural. You say I've committed this wrong, and I ought to do this thing or be damned——"

"No—no—no," murmured Mr. Grey, with a wild movement of his hands of entreaty. "Not that—don't put it so; you hurt me, Trevenna."

"I don't mean to," Trevenna said, with a softening for the first time audible in his harsh voice. "I'm hardly fiend enough, bad as I am, to hurt the only living soul that cares whether mine is lost or saved."

"Trevenna, I need not be the only one; you might yet have love and care about you. It is for your own sake, as well as for the right, I urge this step."

"That's bosh—humbug, my dear fellow!" the other said, in his hardest tone of cynical denial. "I look for nothing of the sort, for absolutely nothing! Let's

have no false gloss on the thing, no senti-
mentality. If I take the step you advise,
I take it because, in spite of all my hard-
ness of heart and badness of life, *something*,
I know not what, struggles within me, and
urges me to make some feeble effort
against wickedness, 'some power not myself that makes for righteousness' which
I cannot formularize or define, but which
you choose to call God, the spirit within
that strives with one's familiar devil, for
what end I know not; or else I do it
because you give me no peace, because
you are fool enough to go on caring what
I am, and what becomes of me—of the
spiritual *me*, that is to say, for the bodily
part of me is judged and condemned to
speedy dissolution with more or less pre-
liminary torture. So, to please you, or
because I have, perhaps, a lurking idea that
you may be right, and that *something* is of
more consequence than even dying, I entertain this idea. Not in the least, my good

Edmund, to patch up my lost and rotten life, or to try to get any satisfaction out of it for myself. It *may* be a tardy act of justice, it may be the girl's right—you say so, and I give you the credit, as I remarked before, of being a moral expert. But in the mess I have made of everything, whatever I do some one must suffer—in this case Geoffrey will. Probably his having vexed me lately makes me—it is so difficult to disentangle one's motives— more willing to do what will cause him to suffer. This girl he fancies will have money, that will pain him for the loss of mine."

"You think, then—you think Geoffrey is in earnest about her? From what I've gathered this will not be his first—his first, what shall I say?"

"*Affaire de cœur?* Not by any means. The fellow's a lady-killer. No; but I fancy there's more in this. I set Hamley on the alert to find out all he could. He

thinks he's caught—pah! I hate the connection! Purse-proud, intriguing, push-
ing mushrooms. I am certain the girl's a
made-up, ogling, flirting, silly fool. I wrote
when I was feeling particularly low and
bad—I don't mind telling *you*, Grey, that
at times I've been rather weak about the
lad, poor Harry's only boy—I wrote, rather
expansively for me, asking him to come
down and see me. I got a slap in the
face, the most indifferent scrawl in the
world, excusing himself because this fool
of a girl had a birthday party! The fact
is, he thinks it is not worth the trouble to
toady me "—his voice was full of the
fiercest, concentrated bitterness—"that I
have no one else to leave my money to,
so that he is free to please himself and
neglect the sour old uncle he does not care
a rap for, though he has got enough out
of him, God knows, so he does not bother
his head to palaver or pretend. You
can't buy affection or gratitude, I suppose.

I've been lavish to him, paid his debts, grudged him nothing. Now, I've never done a thing for you, except plague and make you miserable, and I believe you are idiot enough to *like* me." He ended with a short, crackling laugh, grimmer and sadder than a sob.

"Why, you know I do, Dick," Mr. Grey said, in his low, mild, sincere voice; "there's no doubt, I hope, on that point. But I believe you wrong your nephew. I believe Geoff cares for you; and, though I own his faults, he has a good heart."

"Pshaw! Praise from a man who can go on caring for Richard Trevenna, is worth nothing. Whom do *you* think worthless, pray?"

"Not Geoffrey, at any rate," Mr. Grey persisted, with gentle obstinacy. "I believe the kindest judgments generally turn out the truest. You like to decry yourself; but my opinion of you is a more exact one, I believe, than your own. You have always been your worst enemy, Dick."

" Well, no enemy could have wrought more havoc in my life, I grant you that. Such havoc that there's no making the smallest mend of it. But, as I said before, for the reason I've stated, and because you are the only friend I have in heaven or on earth, I'll do what you want."

" Dick—Dick, old friend—" Mr. Grey was stammering hopelessly, grinding his hands together in sore distress—"don't talk so—your only friend—in heaven —my dear old fellow, you know better— I know better—believe me, I know—I *know*, I say! There *is* a God—a Christ —for you, for me—"

"Ah! Speak for yourself, old man. It's too late to make a reformed character of me. But if anything could ever per-suade me to believe in *anything* better

than this horrible chaos and black misery
of a world, reeling hopelessly from space
to annihilation, it would be that such as
you exist. Don't let's talk like this any
longer for a bit. I'm rather worn out
and exhausted. Here comes tea, the
old woman's comfort, to which I am
reduced. After a cup, and a drop of
cognac, I'll just discuss the next steps
with you. If this thing has to be, you'll
have to carry it through ; I've no energy
left, except when I'm in a rage, and I
dread everything. I leave it in your
hands, old man."

Mr. Grey gave a sort of gasp, expres-
sive of the terror which the prospect of
action gave his timid and, at times,
rather indolent spirit, yet he never dreamt,
terrible as the responsibility was, of
repudiating it. Stronger than fear,
stronger than indolence, stronger than his
desire for calm and peace, was the deep
conscientiousness, the fervent love of right

which dwelt in his inmost heart. He
had no doubts or dimness of vision
as to questions of right and wrong,
the expedient, the convenient, weighed
nothing. A certain course had always
seemed to him straight, his friend had
persistently taken another; now, though
at the eleventh hour, his gentle, but
strenuous remonstrances, the entreaties of
his loving soul, seemed to have at last
produced some effect. He dreaded, un-
speakably dreaded, the mission laid upon
him; but he accepted it. If he had not
had this moral heroism to give him
power, Edmund Grey would have been
nothing but a coward; his frail little
blundering body quailed and shivered,
his stammering tongue refused to do his
bidding often, but his spirit had the only
sort of courage possible to such a nature,
and would face not only death, but the
worst terrors of life, rather than be false
to the inner voice, to which he had

listened so reverently and intently, that it had learnt how to command so as to ensure obedience. He could not talk, however, even in his most exalted moments; now, he could only blink and gasp and stutter in half-inaudible accents, that he would do whatever he could. Trevenna looked at him with a light, half of ridicule, half of amusement, in his sunken eyes, yet he was conscious all the while of a warmth of love and gratitude to which with all other men he was absolutely a stranger. So love is paid by love all the world over, except in the hell that the demons of passion make for themselves, in this unhappy existence of ours.

CHAPTER II.

IT is always trite to talk of the contrasts of life ; but, whether it is so or not, the glaring nature of some will flaunt themselves before us, and force us into cheap moralizing. The scene in which Mr. Trevenna's nephew played his part on that same evening which introduced the uncle to you was of the nature of such violent contrasts. On one side the sombre dim room, which held only pain, regret, and the dreary expectation of worse to come, where the two elderly men talked together in the twilight, and on the other was Geoffrey Trevenna in a brilliantly, yet softly lighted great London drawing-room,

filled with the music of a swinging, plaintive waltz, mixed with the laughter and
gay voices of frivolous young people whose
trade is pleasure, and heavy with the
manifold perfumes of spring flowers and
manufactured essences. It was Viola Field's
birthday dance. Geoffrey was floating
down the room with this same Viola
in his arms, her light slender swaying
figure was close to him ; he heard the
quick beating of her heart ; he was whispering into her little rosy ear; her small
golden-brown curly-locked head, was drooping close to his white shirt front. He
seemed to have a great deal to tell her in
whispers, though she answered little, yet
all amounted to the same foolish story that
has been told and retold for ages. They
were a goodly couple, he a handsome man
of eight and twenty, as dark as he had
a right to be from a Spanish mother,
Harry Trevenna's foreign wife, who had
never lived to see how like her her boy

had grown, with a foreign grace and ease
of manner, an olive complexion, and beautiful dark eyes ; she the sort of girl people
cannot help calling "sweetly pretty," an
exquisitely made, fragile, delicately coloured
piece of porcelain, slight, yielding as a
flower, with a flower's easily destroyed
bloom, with golden-brown hair, and dark
blue eyes ; just the sort of hair and eyes
to complete the charm of the whole picture.
The smallest head set on the slenderest
throat, the slimmest waist, wrist, little white
fingers, she looked the darling of Fortune
and of Nature—born to be spoilt and petted
from her costly cradle upwards. She was,
of course, perfectly dressed ; except that
perhaps her tiny slight throat and arms
were too much bejewelled. Her parents
had not the finest taste in the world, and
loaded her with presents, and to-day was
her twenty-first birthday, so that numbers
of her ornaments were fresh from Bond
Street ; but her dress, or her " frock," as

she always called it, was lovely, shining white silk, like lily leaves, almost bridal in make and texture. Mr. and Mrs. Field, in intervals of hospitality, had time to watch and admire their only child; they never could get used to her delicate loveliness, which was a freak of nature, and not in the least what one would have expected to spring from the parental fountain. Mrs. Field was a very handsome woman, but Viola was not and never would be like her. The mother was full blown, exuberant, her charms "vous sautent aux yeux." Her white neck was as full as the bust of Clytie, and made a beautiful cushion for her diamond necklace. Her high fixed colour needed no rouge, but her piled up frizz of hair had been judiciously brightened as middle age, which cannot be driven off even by rich fashionable ladies, tended to fade it. She was always to be seen and heard as she dragged her brocaded skirts about, with the diamonds

flashing, as she talked and laughed and
fussed round her big rooms. There were
people who admired Mrs. Field very much,
but they were not those who thought her
daughter perfection. Mr. James Field
was something " connected with shipping,"
as people said vaguely. Mr. Trevenna,
and others who hated him, declared he
owned coffin ships, and had been lucky at
the expense of obscure, uncared for lives.
At any rate he was rich, which is generally
all that the world chooses to know, had a
fine big house, and entertained splendidly.
This covered his subtle vulgarity—which
did not consist in *h*'lessness,—his disagreeable expression and insolence to the
unlucky and importunate. Viola was his
only daughter, an heiress, a beauty. Some
said she might have married *anybody*, and
wondered that she was allowed to take up
with young Trevenna, a briefless barrister,
with a very small fortune of his own, and
nothing much to recommend him but taking

manners, a handsome person, and some
expectations from an invalid uncle in
Oxfordshire. But Viola generally had her
own way—at least, so far in her short life,
when her wishes had seldom clashed with
her father's iron will, she had had it, and
he certainly doted on her.

He had just watched her skim past with
her partner, and a smile of satisfaction
at owning such a pretty thing was on his
full clean-shaven lips, when a rather loud,
rather angry bass voice behind him said,
with startling abruptness—

"Are those two *engaged*, Field, or is it
only flirting ?"

A large man, some forty years old, with
close-cropped red hair, and a not ugly, but
heavy and coarse face, was standing at his
elbow, and scowling with red eyebrows at
the young couple.

"Hullo, Lees! You startled me," Mr.
Field said, turning with a not altogether
easy laugh. "Who's engaged? Who's
flirting ?"

"Don't be a humbug, Field. You know well enough I'm speaking about that little girl of yours, and that puppy Trevenna. I can't think how you allow it—she ought to do better. What's Trevenna?"

"My dear fellow, girls will dance, ay, and flirt too, with a handsome young man. There's nothing settled. But Trevenna's well thought of. He could get on at the Bar if he chose. He goes everywhere, and he will have money."

"Pshaw! Wait till he's got it. The old uncle isn't dead yet. Indeed, I believe he isn't old. Don't let Viola throw herself away, that's all." And he turned on his heel and went heavily on.

Mr. Field laughed to himself. "Poor Lees! He wants little Vi himself. If she would have him, I shouldn't object. Ten thousand a year, if he's a penny, and a good-natured chap when he's pleased. But red hair, a stout figure, and forty years won't hold their own against such an outside as Master Trevenna can boast. Poor old Lees! He's certainly gone on little Vi."

Another person was watching Geoffrey Trevenna — a thin, grave, grey-headed gentleman, of subdued and courteous manner. This was Mr. Hamley, Richard Trevenna's legal adviser as well as James Field's; a man born to be the locked depositary of secrets, an unimpeachable lawyer, a chilly but conscientious friend, who pardoned most sins simply because he expected nothing good of any one, who had liked and disliked, but never either hated or loved in all his calm, decorous life. He had come to this dance, however, for a disinterested motive, and was capable of kindness in his cool fashion. He wanted to get a word later on with Geoffrey Trevenna, whom he thought an " agreeable sort of young fellow," and liked —a little—it was out of his way to like *much.*

Unconscious of lawyers, uncles, fathers, or rivals, Geoffrey was making ardent love to Viola. After a few turns, he bore her off into one of the dark, secluded nooks specially prepared for such couples, and there the whole stream poured out.

"You darling! How sweet you look! You are prettier to-night than you ever were—dearer. Don't let's go on like this any longer. I'll have it out with your father. You can tell them. You know, and I know, that I'm over head and ears in love with you, and you are a little bit in love with me. Let us have it settled once and for all, my little sweet. You'll be my wife, won't you, darling pet?"

Viola's brown head inclined to his shoulder. He had his arm round her slender, yielding, trembling figure. Her soft, low, lisping, childish voice murmured that he knew very well—too well—that she *did* care—not a little—a great deal—too much—she was silly——

" Not silly! The wisest, dearest darling
in the world! It isn't silly to care for a
fellow who'd give his life for you. You
might do better, Vi, I dare say. I'm not
up to much——"

"That's nonsense." A flutter of a light
little hand just touched his lips to silence
him, not staying long enough to be kissed.
"You are a great deal cleverer than I
am. I'm nothing——"

"Oh, nothing at all, only the prettiest
pet of a girl; only an heiress! Just see
what your governor has to say on that
point. He'll very likely want to kick me
off the premises."

"Oh no, Geoffrey. He always lets me
have my own way——"

"And that's *me?* You darling!" A
long, fervent kiss was the only climax
possible. Geoffrey was quivering a little
with the ardent passion of his years and
temperament; but he was surprised to
find how Viola trembled. Her whole

slight frame was shaken; she panted a little, and her heart beat audibly. She was too highly strung, too sensitive, too frail an exotic. He was almost afraid of making love to her for the moment. He relaxed the fervent clasp in which she trembled. "My own sweet pet, I will be so good to you, if only I may have you. I'll make you so happy for ever when you are my very own! I'm afraid we shall have to wait awhile; I haven't money enough to marry on. But some day I shall have, and if only they let us be engaged——"

"Oh, they will let me do anything I want! They could never refuse me—on my birthday, too; such a happy, happy birthday! I felt it was going to be when I woke."

"You ought to have been born under a lucky star. You ought never to know anything that is not smooth and sweet and fair, my little darling."

" I couldn't bear to be unhappy," she said softly, with her clinging hands on his. " It always made me ill to cry. No one ever let me. I am afraid I've been dreadfully spoilt."

" Then how have you managed to grow up to be such a jewel? I don't see where the spoiling comes in. You are the kindest, sweetest, tenderest little girl in the world. What more could you be?"

" But then I've never had any trouble or temptation at all. I could not help being kind, for every one has always been kind to me."

" And so they ought to be; so they shall be always. You shall never, never have a cross word or look, if I can shield you. I'll be your slave, your lover, your worshipper always, for ever and ever."

" I don't want a *slave*, dear, I want you to be my lover. I do love to be loved."

"As if one could help it. You pretty, pretty *darling !* "

She paid him for his passionate praises and caresses with soft little coaxing touches, sweet little murmurs, a half-yielding, a half-retreating which set his blood on fire. When he came out again into the world of the ball-room his dark handsome face was burning, his eyes were bright and moist, his heart was beating fast. Even a casual observer might have guessed what stirred him so, a cool, quiet touch and polite well-modulated voice fell on his heated rapture like a dash of cold water. He wheeled round almost fiercely upon the disturber of his reverie, and found that it was Mr. Hamley. The flushed, dark, handsome face was nearly insolent, if the lawyer had been thin-skinned he would have kept the words that had risen to his lips to himself, and been too much offended with the arrogant young fellow to have cared to say them for his benefit. But Mr. Hamley had never been thin-skinned, and in his calm middle age had sedulously cultivated a philosophic composure not to be ruffled by any outward circumstances, which did not trouble the elaborate machinery of his ease.

"You must pardon my detaining you a moment, Mr. Trevenna," the level voice said; "I just wanted to take the opportunity for one word or two. I called at your chambers but you were out, and the clerk did not seem to know when to expect you."

Geoffrey flushed a little, he tried not to look embarrassed—his engagement of the day had nothing at all to do with either law or business, and he felt certain that Mr. Hamley was perfectly aware of the fact. He gave a little contemptuous laugh.

"I did not know you affected ball-rooms, Mr. Hamley. I shouldn't have thought it in your line."

"They are not, decidedly not. I had some business with Mr. Field, and he was good enough to ask me to look in to drink Miss Viola's health, and, as I felt sure I should see you, I spared an hour of my much occupied time."

"Really! That was good of you. Have you anything so important to say to me then, that wouldn't wait another day?"

"There are some things that *won't* wait — a few," Mr. Hamley returned dryly; "death is one of them. You know, of course, that your uncle is in a very precarious state?"

"I know he is in bad health," Geoffrey said, rather startled. "Not that there was anything very imminent. There isn't, is there? I ought to have been told."

"And you have not been? I thought your uncle said he *had* written once or twice, asking you to come down rather urgently. I thought in one of those letters he said there would not long be a chance of seeing him ?"

Geoffrey fidgeted, confused, uncomfortable, inclined to put off any emotion but that which intoxicated his senses. He glanced about him hoping to see Viola, to be distracted from the discomfort of the lawyer's unrelenting matter-of-fact.

"Well I—I believe he said something of that sort. I took it *cum grano;* my uncle is naturally inclined to a gloomy view of himself, and of—of everything and everybody. I did not gather that there was anything very bad the matter."

"No? Well, I am afraid your uncle's medical adviser and Mr. Grey also take the same view of his state. I know nothing more than what they have told me. I thought from what I heard that his health was in that state that no sudden change would be surprising. And as I knew you had not seen him since Christmas I fancied you were hardly perhaps alive to the dangers of his position."

"Not since Christmas! I—certainly I've been to Redwood since then."

"Have you? When?" Mr. Hamley inquired, in a voice so dry as almost to be unbearable.

Geoffrey vainly sought his memory for the imaginary visit. Could it really be four months since he had taken the trouble to throw himself into a first-class carriage for the two hours' journey?

"I thought it had been since then," he muttered, adjusting the faded flower in his coat. Viola gave it him fresh and dewy, he wished flowers would last a little longer, this limp wilted thing somehow vexed his eyes.

"No, I believe I am correct. The last time I was down Mr. Trevenna was speaking a little bitterly of what he called your neglect. I won't say he did not use some stronger word."

"That I am sure he did," Geoffrey said, half smiling. "My uncle's language can be forcible."

"He has been good to you," the lawyer returned calmly.

In another mood Geoffrey would have taken this with careless good-humour, just now it seemed to him disgusting to be held from his newly gained delight, to hear a grim, cold-natured piece of law parchment like this find fault with him. He felt like the wedding guest whom the skinny hand of the ancient mariner coerced.

"I am not ungrateful, sir," he retorted angrily. "I don't exactly see how it affects you!"

"Not in the least, except in your interests," the other returned, with cold indifference. "You will probably quarrel with a reminder that Mr. Trevenna might easily change the disposition of his property. I'll not detain you with

well meant, but evidently unwelcome
warnings or advice."

With a little stiff bow he was turning
on his heel, when Geoffrey, half startled,
put a detaining hand on his arm.

"One moment, Mr. Hamley! I beg
pardon if I spoke rudely—my mind was
a little full of something different."

"So I perceived," Mr. Hamley said,
his thin lips lengthening for a moment
into what was meant for a smile. "It
is easy enough to see with what. You
know, of course, that one of the com-
plaints Mr. Trevenna makes of you has
to do with your intimacy *here?* He is
a man of strong prejudices; he used to
know, and he very much dislikes, our
host."

"I've heard him say so. Of course
I don't want to conceal from you or from
him, when the time comes, that I consider
myself engaged to Miss Field. My uncle
could not dislike *her* if he knew her."

"H'm, Miss Viola Field is very charming, I know, but I fear Mr. Trevenna is hardly the man to change any rooted opinion of his for such a reason. Frankly, he is much displeased with you at present, and I shall think you unwise if you don't try and alter his feelings."

"I will go down and 'see him to-morrow —no, as soon as I possibly can. I will do my best. I have a real regard, whatever any one may think, for my uncle. He has been generous, uncommonly generous to me often, and lenient too. But, after all, Mr. Hamley, I hardly think he would disinherit me. I am his only relation."

Mr. Hamley again uttered his peculiar "hem." He might have been clearing his throat, but the sound seemed to signify a good deal. He looked fixedly and oddly at Geoffrey.

"Well, yes, perhaps—you may say so

—at present—he has no near blood-
relations, no.   But, if I were you, I would
not presume on that, Mr. Geoffrey, to
continue or widen the breach.   Now,
don't let me keep you from your dance
—only think over the earliest day in
which you can pay a visit to your uncle
Richard."

Geoffrey spared an uneasy moment
from his bliss to ponder the meaning
of those last words.   There was more
behind, and something to make him
anxious, if a fellow could be anything but
happy who was fresh from the touch of
Viola's soft endearing caress.   It was
true that he had been so full of her,
and of the delights of his gilded youth,
when to want was to get, that he had
taken very little notice of one or two
bitterly sarcastic sentences in his uncle's
always brief and coldly worded letters.
He had been neglectful and careless of
all those obligations, of every obligation

except that of being happy, and pleasing Viola. He must make it up with the governor—he had been rather a fool; but, cold as he was, his uncle had an affection for him, there was no one else he cared for except old Grey, who was a staunch friend of his, a good, unselfish, disinterested fellow who would not want a halfpenny of his lifelong friend's money. He couldn't possibly go down to Redwood to-morrow; he must see Mr. Field, and get all that over, must be acknowledged as Viola's future husband; but next week he would certainly go and tell his uncle of his engagement. Well, considering his rooted aversion to Viola's father, that might not prove to be a pacifying statement; but, if any one saw her—the pretty, soft-voiced, winsome little darling—it was impossible to resist her! The fiercest misogynist must make an exception in favour of Vi! His thoughts thus returned to their former channel. Geoffrey went gaily to find his partner, and to sip the material and spiritual champagne of life.

" Well Vi, darling, have you enjoyed your ball ? " her mother asked, between her yawns, as, the last guests departed, she prepared to trail heavily upstairs.

" Oh, awfully, mummy ! " the girl said, in the slang of the day, for even Viola could talk slang like the rest. " I never did more in my life."

" You're not overtired ? You look a little worn out."

" N—no—if only I can sleep."

" You must sleep, ducky, or you'll be ill. Here comes papa. Viola looks a bit overdone, doesn't she, papa ? "

He took her chin on his finger and inspected her. " A bit—not much amiss. It was a good ball. You danced a great deal too often to please some folks, with young Trevenna, Vi."

He watched with amusement the blood

rushing to the face he still held up for inspection. He had always enjoyed making his little girl blush. " How many times, missy, eh ? "

" Oh, I don't know, papa. What does it matter ? *You* don't mind ? "

" H'm ! I don't know that. There were one or two who did, anyway, that are worth more than to be sniffed at by a fastidious little minx like you. Just because Trevenna's a good-looking, fine-spoken fellow, who can make a fool of a girl—— "

" Let me go, papa," Viola cried, half irritably, half plaintively, twisting herself from his grasp. " I'm tired ; I want to go to bed."

There was something pathetic in the girl's voice at times—a ring, a minor note which her mother never could hear un-moved. Was it likely she should, when she connected the tone with long nights of watching, with heart-sickening fears and

forebodings, the many times since baby-
hood that Viola had been ill ?   It had
always been Mrs. Field's desire to keep
the rough winds from ruffling a hair of
the child's head.   She was " so delicate,"
as she continued to say long after the
doctors had left off insisting on it, to the
irritation of her husband, who considered
enough had been spent over Vi's health to
start a hospital, and always strongly
declared that there was nothing at all
wrong with it, if her mother didn't fuss so
confoundedly.

" Let her go, papa," she cried too ; " she
is regularly done up.   You can go on at
her about her partners, or anything else,
when she's rested.   Call Firth, love, and
get into bed as quickly as ever you can."

Poor Firth looked far paler and more
tired than her young mistress ; but Viola,
though she had the dormant kindness of a
soft nature, was not brought up to see the
fatigue of a maid.   It would have been a

wild impossibility to have undressed herself after dancing for four hours, or, indeed,
at any time. She was more helpless than
a baby born into the necessities of a
cottage, and servants were paid to unlace,
untie, brush hair, and pull off dainty little
white slippers. There *were* unhappy girls
who had to dress their own hair, pack
their own boxes, and lay out their party
frocks and chiffons. Viola was sorry for
them, and thankful she was born into
another life. She felt altogether thankful,
and flutteringly happy, as she sank into
sleep, into which she fondly but vainly
hoped visions of a dark, ardent face, and
passionate deep eyes might come. As for
Firth she went grumbling to her three
hours' repose with a wish that Providence
had made her the fine lady she was sure
she should have acted to perfection.

CHAPTER III.

" MUMMY dear, I've something to tell you."

Mrs. Field and Viola were dawdling in the mother's cosy sitting-room, after a late breakfast, the morning after the birthday ball. According to the habit of girls who have the most important announcement of their young lives to make, Viola was careful that not even the fond maternal eyes should look into hers as she spoke, swinging the ribbons of her pretty morning wrapper, with down-dropped head, and aimless little white fingers.

" Eh, dear, have you ? " the mother said, on the alert at once, and prepared for what was to follow ; " then there really is something ? "

" Yes, mummy. And you know who it is ? "

" Well, I expect I do. I suppose it's that Trevenna fellow."

I need hardly premise that Mrs. Field's habit of mind and speech were not of the Vere de Vere order. Viola, carefully trained in a very different school, and used to orthodox society, and a shibboleth of a class above their own, was not unaware that both father and mother were at times common in talk, and always so in their views of life ; but she had met with un-bounded indulgence and kindness from them, and shrank with a nervous dread from even mental criticism. But now she was in a state of tension and excitement of mind, which made her irritably fastidious.

" Mother ! " she cried sharply, " don't call him that. Of course it is Geoffrey Trevenna—don't call him ' that fellow ! ' "

"I meant no harm, child," her mother returned apologetically, for she hated to vex this one cherished daughter of hers. "I like him well enough; he's very good-looking and nice, I'm sure. Papa likes him, too. Only, you know, ducky, we can't but feel you might have looked a bit higher."

"Why higher? His family's as old as the hills, while ours "—— Viola shrugged her shoulders expressively. "I know his uncle looks down on us. And he's so popular he might marry anybody."

"No now, Vi dear, that's nonsense. It's money, not family, people think of nowadays. A young barrister, with just a paltry two hundred or so of his own, can't marry well; and, family or no, your father's only daughter isn't to be thought too little of neither!"

"I don't know what his income is—I don't care—but even if you put it on that horrid money question, he will be well off when his uncle dies—he's his heir, and I've heard papa say old Mr. Trevenna has a nice little estate."

"Yes," Mrs. Field drawled thoughtfully, "and it's a fact, I believe, that he can't live long. Of course, if it wasn't for *that*——"

"If it wasn't, I should be engaged to him all the same," Viola cried vehemently, flushing a vivid pink as she did easily when moved. "I would never marry any one else."

"Oh, come now, dearie, be reasonable. You *couldn't* marry a poor man. You think you could; but you don't consider. A girl brought up as you've been, with nothing spared that money could buy, a delicate little thing, too, that could no more rough it than—than—" Mrs. Field searched for a simile, and found one in a cage of tropic birds which hung in the window—"no more than those birds could live out o' doors. I think I see you

living in a bit of a place, with two
servants! Romance is all very well, but
one falls back on comfort as one gets
older, and you could never bear poverty,
Vi, never."

"I shan't have to bear it," Viola returned pettishly, her nerves were all on
edge, her mother had never seemed so
provoking. "Geoffrey won't be poor!
And I am engaged to him, mother,
there's no use talking—— "

"Well, I suppose papa and I have
a word in it too?" Mrs. Field said, a
little resentfully. "Such parents as we've
been to you, Vi!"

Viola's was one of those natures
easily frightened out of wrath, by even
a show of anger. She came on to the
sofa and nestled close to her mother's soft
cushiony form, with a slender arm round
the ample waist, which even the most
elaborate corset would not reduce to
slimness.

"Don't be cross, mummy dear," she coaxed, "there's no question of my doing anything you don't like. Geoffrey isn't poor. You know what he is; but you don't know what he is to me. I'm dreadfully in love with him. I should break my heart if I couldn't have him. I suppose *you* were in love once, mummy?"

A sudden sigh rose and fell within the broad matronly bosom, which had not always been only a white cushion to put diamonds on. Ah, when she was young and tender, when she was a light slip of a girl running wild about the fields at home, she, too, had had her fancies, her palpitations of fear and joy, like Viola, only she had been of tougher fibre and harder training. She had *not* been in love with James Field, though she had made him a good wife, and a capital head to his establishment. She had not quite forgotten the time when she and a curly haired lad of two and twenty had exchanged kisses and twopenny-half-penny rings. Mr. Field's magnificent diamonds and rubies adorned her plump white hands now.

"But love isn't everything," she said aloud, a little sadly, after the moment's silence which she gave to a memory roused by the girl's question ; "take my word for it, Vi."

"It's everything to *me*," Viola returned, in an undertone, which was little more than a sigh.

Her mother touched the soft little baby brown curls on her forehead with a fond hand; she might play the stern matron if Viola were petulant, but she was like wax under caressing touches, when the girl coaxed and wheedled her with her wistful sweet voice.

"We shall have to see what papa says. I suppose Mr. Trevenna is coming to speak to him?"

"Yes, this evening. You must tell

papa first, and get him to be nice. I *must* have my own way, mummy. I always do, you know."

"You always do, indeed, I believe you! If ever there was a spoilt baby, it's you."

" But I've always been good—it's been the very best thing for my bodily and spiritual health. Don't you remember old Dr. Sparkes telling you I couldn't bear hardening and thwarting, like some children? When you made me cry, I was always ill, now wasn't I ? "

"When I made you cry! Whenever did I, pray, miss? I'm sure I learnt my lesson well. It's the day of obedient parents now."

"Well, on the whole, I will say that you've been good and obedient ; but I've been just what I ought, too—the best of girls—now haven't I? Some mothers have a dreadful time of it. You should hear how Flossie and Carrie Lambert speak to their mother, and the life they lead her. I never stand out against you —I never will, unless you are nasty about this."

"That's an easy sort of goodness, when you're never vexed or contradicted!"

"Oh, but I am, often! Not by you— at least, not if you can help it—but I often give up what I want to do, because you say I'm not strong enough for this or that, when I should like to go. And papa is disagreeable and cross enough sometimes, when things go wrong in the city, or his dinner isn't to his taste."

"Ah, well, when all's said and done you haven't much to complain of. Your bed's pretty softly stuffed for you, Vi."

"Yes. But I'm like the princess in the fairy-tale, I feel even the peas under my feather beds. Either I was born so, or I've been brought up to it; but I really can't bear things like some people, dear."

"And do you suppose you'll never

have to ?   However shall you get through life without trouble, Vi ? "

" At any rate, I'll wait till the trouble comes.   If I can't stand it, I can just lie down and die, mummy ; it would be an easy way out of it ! "

" Don't talk so ridiculously," her mother cried, with irritation, though Viola spoke lightly enough.

Into the sheltered luxury of the life they led the ideas of such hideous spectres as poverty, acute suffering, and death might not enter.

She promised to " talk to papa " before dinner, and pave the way for Geoffrey's interview.

Mr. Field came home in the best of tempers, for occult reasons, his wife and daughter supposed, connected with that mysterious business life of which they knew nothing, only seeing its fruition in a plentiful crop of cheques.   He declared Viola was made a fool of by a pair of

handsome eyes and a lot of soft sawder;
but since she'd set her heart on the fellow,
he supposed he must allow it to be an
engagement. *He* didn't mind keeping the
child at home, for of course it could not
end in a marriage till young Trevenna
came in for his uncle's property. It
wasn't the match he should have chosen;
but girls would have their own way.

So he was not ungracious to Geoffrey,
though a little too inquisitorial and patron-
izing to suit a proud temper. Geoffrey
had to own that his profession brought
him in nothing when his chambers and
clerk were paid; that he only had two
hundred a year absolutely of his own, and
his uncle allowed him the same. Of
course he knew he couldn't ask Viola to
marry him on that, but they might be
engaged; he had expectations.

"Ay. How much now *has* your
uncle?"

Geoffrey felt irritated, but was careful

not to show it. Young men, even when
proud and hasty-tempered, are apt to be
wonderfully complaisant to the fathers of
their beloved.

"Between four and five thousand, I
believe."

"And you are actually his heir?"

"He has, as far as I know, no other
relations. I have every reason to expect
that I am."

"And he can't live long. H'm, well,
I couldn't let my girl marry a man who
wouldn't settle five hundred pounds a
year on her. I would allow her the same
during my life. She will come in for a
good income when I die. I suppose I
must allow it to be considered an engagement; but frankly, Trevenna, I don't
think Vi is doing as well for herself as she
ought."

"No, sir, I dare say you don't,"
Geoffrey said, with studied self-command.
"I quite agree with you; but she cares

for me, you see—that goes for something—and no man could be fonder of her than I am."

"Oh yes," Mr. Field returned, with good-humoured cynicism. "That's all very nice; but love don't pay a woman's milliner's bills. Viola's been expensively brought up, and she's not going to marry to be less comfortable than she is, if I can help it. But we'll let it be called an engagement, since nothing else will satisfy either of you. You can go and spoon her now, if you like."

Geoffrey was glad to be dismissed on any terms. The one thorn in the half-blown rose of his love was the individuality of Viola's father. Her mother, pronounced as she was, and by no means after his heart, was bearable. Her florid good nature and unbounded affection for Vi covered her sins of omission and commission; but Mr. Field was secretly abhorrent to him. His impatient, fastidious temper, all the inherited instincts and habits of gentlehood, revolted against the unblushing vulgarity of soul, the un-deviating self-sufficiency of the purse-proud, rampant Philistine, to whom Viola had the misfortune to belong. But the readiest way to put the vexation of James Field's existence out of his mind was to see Viola and to revel in her half-coy, half-yielding sweetness, to triumph in her charm, and to adore the exquisite finish which her very frailty accentuated.

He had his brand-new, sparkling mar-quise ring ready for her tiny third finger, which needed no ring to be lovely, with its pink, almond-shaped little shell of a nail, as delicately pretty as a flower-petal. Those small, white, useless hands were one of Viola's decided beauties. Geoffrey loved to see them on his own broad palm, or stroking the rough, dark sleeve of his coat.

Like most men who have a good

opinion of themselves and a decided will, his ideal of womanhood was small, refined, caressing, flower-like. He did not want a strong-minded, intellectual, universally accomplished woman.

Viola was not stupid, but either indolence of mind or physical inability made her singularly ungifted in the ordinary talents of womankind. She could neither sing, play, nor paint, though she knew how to dance perfectly, which perhaps did as well. She had the merest smattering of knowledge on any subject; never opened a book of more lofty aim than a society novel, and would have been sorely puzzled to do anything more elaborate with her needle than some little fashionable frippery which passed for fine work. What did it matter? They could always pay servants to "do things," and Viola in herself, without one talent beyond dancing and dressing to perfection, and being able to hold her own in lively small talk, was just adorable. To have added anything would be mere painting the lily. At any rate she was not many undesirable things that some girls are. She was a delicate coquette ; but there was no brazen fastness, no abandon about her, which men take advantage of for their amusement, but—if they are refined in mind—loathe in reality when the time for choosing seriously comes. Viola neither swore, smoked, nor romped, as many of her compeers did. There was always a subtle fragrance of innocence about her ; she was never either unladylike or unwomanly. Something vaguely pathetic and wistfully appealing, though she had never had a sorrow in her life greater than the death of a pet dog, added to the indefinable fascination which had laid hold of Geoffrey Trevenna's very heart-strings. He could have refused her nothing when her light, clinging hands were on his shoulders, and her soft, wild-violet eyes looked into his with something of sadness in them which facts had never justified. The faces of perfectly happy people have sometimes that indefinite pathos which now and then means a fore-boding, but more often is a mere cunning trick of Mother Nature's fingers. On the other hand, a homely, stolid countenance is often the mask which hides a woeful heart.

After the usual trivialities of love-making, which are so uninteresting to everybody outside of them, had filled up an hour or so of that first evening's per-mitted bliss, Geoffrey told Viola inci-dentally of Mr. Hamley's reproaches and vague hints of more to follow, and de-clared he must lose no time in running down to Redwood to make his peace.

" Let me see, to-morrow's Saturday. Perhaps I'd better spend Sunday with the governor."

Viola's eyes were overshadowed as by a tragedy.

" Oh, dearest, not to-morrow—not Sunday. Go next week. To-morrow I've set my heart on driving you with my new ponies—papa's birthday present; and on Sunday we expect some people I should like you to know—my great friend, Connie Millington. You'll not go to-morrow, Geoffrey ? What can one day matter ? "

" I expect old Hamley would say it did."

" But not really ; it could not make any difference. We are only just engaged. It would be too naughty of you to go away directly. Say Monday will do, dearest."

Who could resist the appealing eyes, the pouting baby mouth she made ? Not Geoffrey Trevenna, only twenty-eight years old, madly in love, and just put in possession of all this sweetness. Monday would do, he decided, and he would try the new ponies to-morrow instead of going down to do his duty, dismally, in a melancholy, half-empty old house, full only of suffering, dreariness, and discontent.

CHAPTER IV.

THE next day fickle April suddenly
leapt into sunshine, warmth, and
floweriness. The grim old giant London
smiled and looked positively beautiful in
the golden air, under a sky of almost
Italian blue. The trees in their first pale
green robes pretended to be young and
gay, and to have no prevision of blacks
or fogs to come ; the parks were gorgeous
with tulips and hyacinths ; the girls looked
like walking flowers. It was enough
pleasure to be young and alive, and when
in addition one is just in the first flush of
permitted love—well, Geoffrey was glad to

forget that Redwood and duty still remained in the immediate future. There
were two days of the garden of Eden first.

Viola had some shopping to do, she
announced, and Geoffrey must drive her
in the charming little pony-phæton which
her father had given her with a pair of
ravishing little grey beasts, with tails long
enough to gladden a woman's heart. She
came down, as he waited on the doorsteps
watching the turn-out, in a new elaboration
of the Court dressmaker who condescended
to take her orders, though she was not a
member of the aristocracy. The masculine mind could only grasp that it was
a sort of cunning combination of the very
colours of spring—primrose and hyacinth
blue—and that she looked like an embodi-
ment of the April day in living lovely flesh
and blood. It might—probably would—
be cold again to-morrow, and then Viola
would cover herself with furs and velvet ;
but to-day was warm, was almost summery,

and she could not but be in keeping with
it all.

"Aren't they beauties?" she cried gaily,
descending the steps, with the big footman
gazing approvingly after her from above.
"It was a lovely present of the old dad's,
wasn't it?"

"Lovely. I was just thinking how the
whole thing matched—you and the ponies
and that new smart frock and hat. I feel
like a blot on this fairy-queen turn-
out."

"Nonsense. *You* look lovely too; but
your buttonhole is not quite *chic*. Here's
another I've made for you. Put it in.
There, now you must drive. I like to be
lazy best; and, though I can do it when
I choose, and they are charming little
fellows, I always do feel a wee bit nervous
when I have reins in my hands."

"Oh, I'll drive, if you wish, only you
would look prettier doing so. Are you
comfortable? Are you quite sure you shall

be warm enough? That delicious costume seems rather airy for April."

"You are as bad about coddling me as mummy! I am perfectly warm. I've piles of things on."

"Well, you always look, you know, as if a breath would blow you away. You are made to be coddled."

"Appearances are deceptive. It would take a stiff breeze to do it."

"And I always mean to stand between you and a rough wind, little sweet. 'My plaidie to the angry airts,' etc."

"Well, it's not bad to have some one between one and the wind, I own. Perhaps being thin and looking delicate have their advantages. What a perfectly splendid day it is, and how utterly jolly it is to be alive in it."

"And to have some one driving you who is head over ears in love!"

"Well, that, too, has its advantages. One of them is that chocolate is an offering appropriate to lovely beings. That is a delightful chocolate shop there, Geoffrey, and I am out of sweets."

" You would like to stop for some ? "

" Please. That kind you gave me last."

The little pony-carriage was drawn up at a fascinating French bon-bon shop, and Geoffrey parted easily with half a sovereign. Then there was the Park to cross, a dressmaker's to call at, where he waited till he was tolerably tired and the ponies fidgety; then a stationer to interview about the last thing in ornamental notepaper, some gloves to purchase, and then Viola declared she was tired of jumping in and out, and would turn into the Park again for an unbroken drive.

"Oh, but I've forgotten mother's order to leave at Fortnum and Mason's. I must do that first. You can take it in and save me, Geoffrey. I'll hold the ponies."

" I had better get some one; they are rather restless."

"Oh no ; you won't be two seconds."

Accordingly Geoffrey entered the shop, which was crowded, so that he had to wait a minute to deliver Mrs. Field's note. Directly he had done it, he was aware of some sensation and scuffle by the door, an exclamation of dismay, a cry, "They've run away!" a scutter of hoofs. His heart stood still; but he was outside in an instant. The ponies, fretted by flies, and tired of standing, had begun to fidget and move impatiently; and Viola, who could never overcome timidity with horses, though she had been used to them from her childhood, had jerked the reins with too nervous and uncertain a hand. The little things reared and plunged off into the throng of the street. A good many unavailing attempts were made to stop and hold them ; a dangerous accident seemed imminent, when it was averted, oddly enough, by a woman—a girl—who made a bold dash forward, threw herself in front of the ponies, seized their heads, and held on with a grip of strange intention and power, as if she meant, whatever happened, to fling herself between the other girl in the carriage, who had fallen back as white as death, loosing the reins, and what seemed her probable destruction.

In a moment Geoffrey was there too, and had taken hold of the quivering ponies, with a quick " Thank you," and the briefest glance before he gave his attention to Viola, who was on the point of fainting. One glance gave him, however, a tolerably vivid picture of a tall, strong-looking, young figure, lissom and well knit, of a pair of large clear grey eyes, a firm set mouth, and a long thick twist of light brown hair, which had been shaken out of its fastening, and surprised him by its length. "She looks like Britomart," he thought, in that moment, recalling some picture he had seen of the woman-knight. As soon as she found herself no longer necessary, the girl let the ponies' heads go, and stepped back on to the pavement. In another moment she seemed to have disappeared. Ashamed of his unmeaning scanty expression of gratitude, Geoffrey turned from quieting the ponies and consoling Viola to offer some rather stronger one, and found that Britomart was gone.

"A plucky girl, by Jove, sir," a by-stander said. "If she hadn't been as quick as lightning, and as brave as she was quick, I'm afraid your young lady would have had a nasty accident."

Geoffrey briefly assented. He was somehow vexed to think that it was a chance passer-by, and a *girl*, who had risked her life for his Viola. It ought to have been his opportunity! But he had not much time to waste on vexation or on any speculations about Viola's preserver, he was much too full of Viola herself, whose frail nerves were in a most shattered condition, and who had only just escaped fainting. He took her into a chemist's shop, where salts, sal volatile, petting, and a few hysterical tears relieved her. A pale pink came back into her white little face, she declared, with a feeble attempt at a laugh, that she was all right—no, she would not go home in a cab, nor in any way but with the ponies—little darlings; it was her fault, not theirs! They only started and swerved a little, and she had foolishly jerked the reins, in a fright. If Geoffrey drove she should be perfectly comfortable; she wanted only to get home and have some tea. Geoffrey was a little afraid of a relapse, but Viola's perfect trust in him seemed to reassure her, and she was soon looking and talking almost like herself, only paler than before the fright.

"Who stopped them? I couldn't see anything but a whirl and throng of faces," she asked, as they drove along at a very steady pace.

"It was a girl," Geoffrey answered briefly. "I only just had a glimpse of her, and before I could make out much, she was gone."

"Gone! And no one even thanked her!"

"Oh, I thanked her, in a vague, perfunctory sort of way. I was too full of you, my sweet."

"It seems horribly ungrateful. How could a girl be so strong and brave? Was it a common girl?"

"No, I think not. I tell you I hardly took her in, only that she was very plainly dressed but rather fine-looking, and like Britomart."

"Who was Britomart?" Viola asked, raising her delicate eyebrows in surprise. "I never heard of her. What a queer name."

Geoffrey smiled, it was not new to him to find that his pretty Viola was profoundly ignorant of English literature, and though she often *looked* like a living poem, had small acquaintance with any poetry but " Hymns Ancient and Modern," and a very little Tennyson.

" Britomart was a girl knight, and went about the world fighting with evil creatures. Have you ever heard of Edmund Spenser and the ' Faërie Queene ' ? "

" N—no—I don't think I have," Viola answered dubiously. " I may have done at those tiresome literature lessons at school. It was an allegory, wasn't it ? I detest allegories."

" So do I—unmitigated by poetry—but I choose to think of Una, Amoret, and Britomart as real beings, not as abstract virtues. *You* are an Amoret — such creatures as men love, not these warrior maidens."

" I think I've seen a statue, or a picture,

or something of Una with a lion, but of
course I never could read dull old poems.
I'm terribly ignorant, Geoff dear, I know
—the most frivolous, unintellectual of
girls!"

"And the darlingest. Never mind
about the 'Faërie Queene.' I suppose
honestly, lots of people who pretend to
being literary find it a bore. But I'm
sorry to have been ungrateful to this
Britomart. I couldn't help it, she disappeared somehow. It was an odd thing,
with all those men about, that a woman,
and a young woman, should be the one
effective person to avert a catastrophe.
Oh, Vi, what it might have been!" He
looked at her almost hungrily, with something of a vision of terror in his eyes.

It flashed across him what another
minute might have done, of how he might
have found her with the life crushed out
of her fragile little form, no tender
plaintive voice to answer him, no wistful

blue eyes to dwell on his with conscious answer to his passion.

She nestled close to him. "What is the good of fancying things, Geoff? If we begin going into possibilities we shall be always anxious and wretched. I am not killed; I'm not hurt. You've got me, I've got you; and we are the happiest two in London—say we are!"

"I'm only sure there isn't a happier man there. But one can't help imagining sometimes——"

"Yes one can, if one tries; I never do. I am very matter-of-fact, and the present does for me, since it is always a delightful present."

"Matter-of-fact! *You*, with your face and those sad eyes of yours, that always seem to be looking for something sweeter and rarer than life can bring."

"I can't help my face and my eyes. I am afraid I am a fraud, and they are impositions. I get the credit for being all sorts of things I'm not, because I look delicate, and have rather heavy lids, and large pupils to my eyes. I'm not poetical, or sad, or yearning, or anything that's interesting, I assure you. I'm quite satisfied with myself and you, and life altogether. I was born under a lucky star. I've always had everything I want, and I believe I always shall."

" I hope you may," Geoffrey muttered. He was a man of moods, easily swayed to exaltation or depression, and now that Viola had revived like her namesake, when the sun shines after a shower, he felt somehow vaguely depressed and foreboding, the interview at Redwood loomed uninvitingly before him. Viola's words, he knew not why, struck on him with a sort of jar, a misgiving; he did not quite know whether to believe her or her face, with that mysterious hieroglyph which Nature writes on some, the sign manual of sorrows to come.

His spirits were not raised by finding that Mr. Field and Mr. Lees had both come home early to tea, as the latter had brought some tickets for a much-talked-of new operetta.

Mr. Lees, the red-headed, burly Dives, who had carried on a deliberate blunt sort of courtship to Viola by means of such offerings, by rather too open staring, and compliments which Geoffrey did not think she disliked enough, was repugnant to the fastidious young fellow, whom Mr. Lees coarsely described as a "d——d sight too stuck up to suit my book!"

Geoffrey could not understand how Viola could tolerate his gross attentions, and he was always irritated by the fact. In truth Viola cared nothing at all for Mr. Lees, who personally was unpleasant to her ; but the spoilt darling, the princess of a luxurious middle-class affluence, liked compliments, flowers, French sweets and trinkets, whatever their source, as a canary bird likes his lump of sugar. It was too bad that the evening to which he had looked forward as a delicious *solitude-à-deux*, should be spent at a flaring, noisy theatre, in company with Mr. and Mrs. Field, and "that brute Lees." But it would be worse to go away and sulk by himself, for he should be tortured by fancying how "that brute" would stare at Viola, and tell her point blank how pretty she looked, and that she might not resent it. So he had to make up his mind to the inevitable, and accept his first renunciation, since he had been Viola's acknowledged lover.

Viola's mother soon discovered, in one rapid maternal scrutiny, that she looked pale, and the story of the fright and escape was told rather reluctantly, since Viola knew how her father would take it. It was his way to be angry always when either fate or some one's fault made anything happen that he did not like, even when there was no one in particular to be angry with. He began by swearing he wished he hadn't been fool enough to buy those confounded little beasts—they'd better be shot at once ; then, as Viola eagerly declared they were not in the least to blame, he glowered on Geoffrey.

"You oughtn't to have left her like that, Trevenna. Vi was always a fool with the reins. It wasn't safe. I should have thought you'd have had the sense to know that."

" I'm sorry I did," Geoffrey said politely, but with displeasure beneath the outward civility of manner.

Again Viola eagerly interposed. She had wished it, she had said she would not have any one to hold them. It was only for a few seconds.

So this passed, though Geoffrey chafed under the sensation that both Mr. Field and his friend were offensive in their manner to him. Indeed, James Field did

not, at that moment, at all object to producing this impression. His good humour
of last night was over, his friend Tom
Lees' reception of the news of Viola's
engagement had put him out. It had
been a very angry one. Lees had sworn
and blustered, had declared it was a d—d
shame that a nice girl was thrown away
like that! He'd have married her himself,
and settled a thousand on her—it was
what he meant, and he'd have spoken
before, only he never supposed Field
would have been fool enough to allow his
only daughter, and a deuced pretty one
too, to be engaged to a penniless barrister!

These two men were what the world
calls friends, certainly intimates, privileged
to call each other fool or ass at pleasure.
James Field had a great respect for Tom
Lees' money and shrewd head for business, and liked him for a boon companion
at the Derby or a club-dinner, and would
have been delighted to have owned him

for a son-in-law, though there was not ten years difference in their age, but he could not thwart his girl, who always would have her own way, and he feebly remonstrated against the word "penniless;" it wasn't so bad as that, and Trevenna was his uncle's heir.

"Bah!" retorted the angry Tom Lees, "compared to you and me, Field, the fellow *is* penniless, and as for expectations," —he blew them away with a snort of contempt—"see your money down, I say; don't wait for dead men's shoes. You've made a mess of Viola's prospects, that's the plain fact, and ought never to have allowed it. Let's hope the thing won't come off."

After this both Mr. Field's and Mr. Lees' attitude towards Geoffrey may be understood. Viola and her mother did their best, as women do, by a great deal of would-be easy, lively chatter, to cover the uncomfortableness of the situation.

Mrs. Field was wont to tell her daughter, confidentially, when "papa was very cross," and must be humoured, or there would be a "bother." They had no illusions about "papa," though both were fond of him.

"Who stopped the carriage? We haven't heard that," Mrs. Field said, pressing Viola to eat plenty of hot scone, to revive her after her fright, something on Mrs. Jennings' principle of "old Constantia" being good for disappointed affection.

"It was a girl, fancy that!" Viola said.

"And what did you do for her? Of course you gave her something?"

Geoffrey laughed a little. "She wasn't the sort of girl to give money to, Mrs. Field. As far as I could tell she was a lady, but I hardly saw her before she was gone."

"Dear, how odd! She must have been a strong-minded sort of woman."

"Strong armed, at any rate. She was very prompt and brave."

"Well, it makes me just shiver to think of what might have happened. But all's well that ends well; she's safe and sound, thank Heaven. We dine earlier than usual for the play, Geoffrey. You'd better be back here by seven, if you'll come too. Will you?"

"Why, of course, mummy!" Viola cried; and, though Mr. Lees was not cordial, he did not say that the box would not hold the five of them.

So Geoffrey spent a rather unideal evening in not the best of tempers, and was only consoled by one moment's clasp and kiss to reward him for the ordeal of seeing Tom Lees stare at Viola, and to try not to quarrel too openly with him for doing so. Away from her he could be philosophical, and recognize that he had not the exclusive right of admiring her; but he had neither calmness of temper nor habit of self-forgetfulness to enable him to stand even such rivalry as this without irritation. Like Viola, he had been so far a spoilt child, and had not learnt to share his sweets with the world in general.

CHAPTER V.

MR. TREVENNA of Redwood had been, though not materially worse, suffering enough during those blissful first days of Geoffrey's engagement, which fleeted by for him while they lingered on in leaden cruelty for his uncle, to be more than usually irritated by the continued neglect which galled his morbid, angry, and unhappy heart. Each day that week he had expected Geoffrey to come, if not, at least to write; but he heard nothing of him. Only rumours reached him that Geoffrey was perpetually at the Fields'.

"He doesn't care a straw whether I am in tortures, alive, or dead," he growled out

to his friend Grey on the Sunday afternoon, when he paid his usual melancholy
visit, "except that dead he thinks I shall
be of more value to him than alive."

"N-n-no, d-don't say that," Mr. Grey
stammered, as usual incoherent but eager
in apology. "Geoffrey is n-not, n-not—— "

"Not what? Even you stutter over a
defence," his friend retorted, with a little
smile of contempt; "and if *you* can't find
a good word for him, God forgive him, for
no man could."

"Not heartless; you know that, Trevenna."

"I don't know it. If you mean by
heart what is really sentimental boy's fancy,
that the fool is always falling in love with
some pretty, empty-headed noodle, I dare
say he has *heart* enough; but for the man
who reared him, spent and was spent on
him, cared for him, grudged him nothing,
he has none. If I suffered the tortures of
the damned—and God knows at times I

can't imagine much worse—he would not trouble so long as he can get his pleasure out of his youth and my money."

"You are hard on him."

"I am just. I know him. He is selfish, self-indulgent, lazy. Well, he has determined me—you began the idea—his conduct has made me bound to carry the project through."

"Don't do from anger to Geoffrey what you would not from abstract right and justice."

At moments the moral force of character which underlay the apparently plastic gentleness of the shy, undecided little man moved him to real dignity, which was almost stern in its rectitude and truth. These, what he called "spasms of firmness," in his usually yielding friend, were never without effect on Richard Trevenna. The men were oddly contrasted—the one who seemed all harsh, cynical strength had a deeper current of weakness than the other with his mild, almost tremulous indecisiveness of manner. The reason was in the innermost source of action. Love needs the truest strength, and love had been turned to hate in the depths of Trevenna's tossed and tortured soul.

" Don't inquire too far into motive, Grey," he said, with an effort, after a mirthless laugh ; " they are mixed enough in an old sinner like me. Anyway, I have made up my mind. I have given Hamley instructions to write to—to Mrs. Hall, and appoint a meeting. You will go with me to town for the purpose. I must have your help through with it, since you instigated it. It is a hateful business, part farce, part tragedy ; but I suppose it must be gone through with while my strength holds out. The whole of life just now is a mere ghastly nuisance, but good times and bad times and all times pass over."

"Don't let that miserable sentence be your only consolation, Trevenna. You will be doing right; there will be a reward and peace beyond these voices."

"I know *you* think so. It's a vast Perhaps. But I shall rest—I shall rest."

"And you may find this a comfort, after all, in the end. Do let me urge that view of it once more, Dick."

"No, no; I tell you no, as I told you before. I'll have no strange woman about me at the last, no one but my old friend, my good old Edmund, to be priest, comforter, companion, what you will—only the one person who cares and has always cared for me. Let paid hirelings do the rest of the disgusting business of stripping off these old rags of mortality. The old feeling, if it ever were anything real, which I doubt, is dead and buried these twenty years. I wouldn't even try and raise its ghost, and I have no natural affections, no yearning for domestic love and all the rest of the humbug. I will just do the thing as a matter of formal duty. I bring no sentiment to bear on it; don't suggest that idea any more to me, Edmund. Neither you nor any other creature can make anything out of this remnant of life, which has been ugly and miserable so long."

" And whatever you do, you'll not be unjust to Geoffrey ? "

" I won't leave him penniless," the other returned grimly. " I promise no more. To have to work and make his way would be the best thing for him. Besides, unless I'm much mistaken, James Field won't bestow his precious daughter on any dis-inherited man; that would be a blessing in disguise, as pious folks say, for Master Geoff. No doubt he'll be cut up; no doubt he'll hate my memory. I can't help that, but I'll benefit him against his will."

The following day, with a post-card to

prepare for his arrival, Geoffrey Trevenna paid his long delayed visit to his uncle. He had managed to make engagements for the next day, which could not possibly be broken, so that his ordeal was not a long one, but he found it severe.

For months past, since his malady and secret sufferings had increased, his uncle had grown more severe, harsh, and un-sympathetic, more inclined to sneer at and criticise every word, to find fault with every action. In former years, though he had often fallen into disgrace, and had been on uncomfortable terms with him, there had been intervals of good fellowship, when Mr. Trevenna had been not only generous but almost genial, when he had been amused and amusing, and in such seasons, the young fellow had easily forgotten and forgiven the disagreeable moods, and been fond of the changeable, cynical, yet not unkindly uncle, to whom it came easy to give, and who was not a severe censor of morals. They had had pleasant times together, the memory of which was still green, but they were all memories now. The bitter, hard, almost cruel temper had become the habitual aspect which Geoffrey met. Both men had too much inward likeness to get on well, at those times when friction and vexing opposition came between them. Both had the thin-skinned, proud temper of the old Cornish Trevennas; both had a mixture of passion and critical fastidious-ness, which made each apt to annoy and alienate the other. Geoffrey had now all the advantages of youth, warmth of blood, kind-heartedness, and love of life, which perhaps Richard had once known before the crust of morbid hatred and disgust of self, and of the world around, had grown over his better nature. The very likeness, with this contrast of conditions between them, angered the elder man, and gave an edge to his disapproval and resentment. He received him with a mixture of freezing civility, and bitter though veiled displeasure, thanking him for at last bestowing a few hours on a dull hole like Redwood, and the old rat who snarled within it. Geoffrey was too full of himself to take much trouble to bring his uncle into a better humour. He supposed it was illness that made him so ill-tempered, and was sorry, in a light easy sort of way, that he suffered; but young men of twenty-eight, with the warm blood of health and happiness like sparkling wine within them, don't deeply sympathize, as a rule, with pain and decay. He meant to show feeling, but he could not help betraying that he was all the while absorbed in his own sensations. Living in the high summer of his triumphant love, how could he realize the winter of discontent which made the other's mental atmosphere? And while Richard Trevenna declared to himself, as well as to others, that he wanted no pity, and believed in no sympathy, he had in reality a nature that craved solace of this kind, and that had starved and grown sour from need of it. What puzzles and complications are within every one of us, unless, as in Edmund Grey's case, self is dropped as a useless encumbrance impeding the powers of the heart! This simplifies a disposition marvellously. Both the Trevennas were by no means unselfish men, and collisions were inevitable. Geoffrey postponed his piece of news which he knew would not be a welcome one, till close upon the time of leaving, when he nonchalantly informed his uncle, in a casual sort of way, that he was just engaged to Miss Viola Field.

" I know you don't care for her governor —no more do I, to tell the truth; but you'd be certain to like Viola if you knew her."

" You think so ? Why ?" his uncle asked,

with chilling coldness, his deep-set, angry dark eyes emphasising his antagonism.

Geoffrey coloured, and fidgeted with the ornaments on the mantelshelf, against which he leant. He tried for an unsuccessful little laugh.

"Why? Well, because she's charming, of course."

"It is to be presumed you find her so, or you would hardly have looked out for a wife in a family like that. The most disgusting type of purse-proud, insolent bourgeois. People whose veins run money —a man whose father was a low pawn-broker and usurer!"

"We needn't go back to a girl's grand-father. Mr. Field isn't an ideal sort of man, I allow. I don't even stand out that he's a perfect gentleman; but that makes no difference to her."

"Oh, doesn't it?" with a single knocked laugh, as grating as rusty iron.

"No, I say it doesn't!" Geoffrey

reiterated, with an attempt not to show anger. "Viola herself is a pearl, her manners would suit the daughter of a Duke, she is pretty, refined, more than ordinarily so. I'm only speaking of externals."

"Oh, you imagine you have found a pearl. Did any boy ever think he'd made a blunder yet? It is hardly to be supposed that these supposititious charms, which I have to take on trust, will reconcile me to a match which links you with people I despise and detest. I tell you I knew James Field when he was young. I knew his father—the man turned money-lender and ruined a fellow I cared for. D'you know how this same James Field has made his money?"

"No; I don't know, nor care," Geoffrey returned sullenly. "His money's nothing to me. You don't suppose I want her for that?"

"No. I grant you that much. I don't

think you're a knave, only a fool. If you marry a girl out of that family you will be a fool of the purest strain."

"Most people are, according to you, Uncle Dick."

"Yes, they are; I've more and more reason every day to think so. I don't exclude myself. I was a fool of fools to expect anything of you but ingratitude and idiotic selfishness. I can't go on talking or listening to you—I'm not up to it. Mind, I'm not going to die yet—don't hope it—and mind this too, I can leave my property as I choose, and I do *not* choose that it shall go to James Field's son-in-law. Don't say I hold out any false hopes to you; I'm not merely raving, I mean what I say. I absolutely and entirely disapprove of your marrying this girl."

He was panting for breath, and the perspiration of pain was on his livid face. In spite of strenuous efforts after cynical indifference and absence of emotion, he

could not help the access of fits of violent
anger and agitation which shook the
shattered foundation of his frame like a
moral earthquake.

Geoffrey was thankful for an interruption.
He chose to attribute the violent threats
and show of anger to physical causes.
The poor old man was so weak that his
temper had become ungovernable ; it never
had been good, and he hated thwarting.
He probably didn't mean half what he
said. If he could be persuaded to see
Viola he would give in. In old days, a
pretty girl had sometimes produced an
effect upon his uncle, and brought out the
courteous, chivalrous manner which had
made him fascinating to women in his
youth, though neither courtesy nor chivalry
had ever gone deep, they were habits
formed from his bringing up, from the
traditions of the fine old family to which
he belonged and nothing more, for he had
never felt the real respect and reverence

for women which Mr. Grey had, but had been too awkward to make as effective as Trevenna's unreal show of them. It wouldn't do to bother one's self about the threat which probably meant nothing but an expression of bodily discomfort. He said good-bye to his uncle with an air of good-humoured indifference which filled the cup of Richard Trevenna's wrath. He said nothing, not even to his one only confidant, beyond the bare announcement that Geoffrey had told him of his engagement, but he made his preparations deliberately for a journey, short enough, and as easy as money can make a journey now ; but still a formidable affair to an invalid who had not left his house, except for a short drive, for months, and involving not only bodily fatigue and discomfort, but a mental effort painful to an extraordinary degree to a man at once sensitive and scornful of sentiment, bitterly dissatisfied with every condition of life, and profoundly hopeless in every outlook for the future ; a man, too, to whom any intercourse had grown difficult, and any which involved an abandonment of reserve in the smallest degree hateful. But a mixed set of motives and feelings, good and bad, urged him on, and he did not relent to his own shrinking as from something loathsome and intolerable.

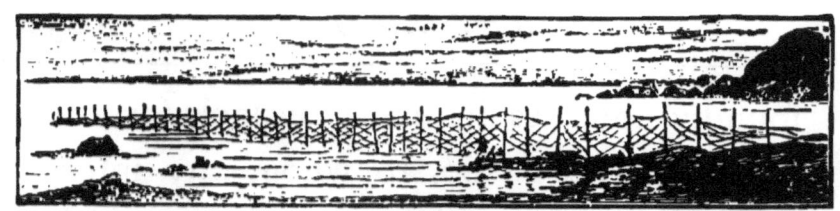

CHAPTER VI.

ABOUT twenty miles from London, on the Surrey side, not far enough from the great devourer to be free of a certain suburban taint, though dull enough for any remote district, there is a little town, or large village, where the remains of the past still linger in a church of some antiquity though no special beauty, and a few old-fashioned houses, but which the jerry builder has invaded with stucco villas and attempts at Queen Anne architecture. The country round, though spoilt in some places by brick-fields, and by a paper factory which has ruined what was once a pretty dell and stream, has its prettiness.

There is a pleasant common, gorgeous in autumn in purple and gold, where the sunsets are beautiful ; and on the borders of this common, outside the small, uninteresting town are a few scattered houses and cottages. In one of these three women lived with whom our story has to do. There was no quieter household in Copsley—only a middle-aged, stout, apathetic-looking mother with the remains of beauty long dimmed and blurred by that inexorable spoiler, Time, who is only baffled by the highest and most exquisite type of womanhood ; a daughter a year or two over twenty, and an elderly, thin, frosty-looking servant, who seemed to find in perpetual work a panacea for the woes of life. Scarcely a soul entered the doors. Mrs. Hall seemed to have no friends. The doctor, the vicar, the vicaress, and one or two benevolent old ladies who "didn't like not to be friendly with their neighbours," were the only people who had penetrated into the small low-ceiled sitting-room where Mrs. Hall sat endlessly knitting, where Penrose drew and worked. It was nearly twenty years since these three took up their abode at Heathside Cottage. Penrose was then a tiny girl with great, grave grey eyes and a thick mane of golden-brown hair. Mrs. Hall was young, handsome, and then comparatively slender, but not less quiet and lymphatic—a shy, reserved, silent woman who, as her neighbour, Miss Babb, declared, was either too frightened or too stupid to have a word to say for herself. Miss Babb, brisk, alert, and deeply concerned in parochial affairs, was at first pleased with the idea of new neighbours, she had called as soon as the cottage presented a settled appearance.

Miss Babb was a spinster, at that time over fifty, who had spent her half-century in the small centre of the pettiest kind of life that it is possible for a woman to move

in. Her appetite for the concerns of her
neighbours, and for a collection of well-
authenticated facts regarding them, grew
with what it fed on. The tiny scandals
and racy secrets of a village life were her
books, her luxuries, her joys. She was
not utterly odious because her insatiable
curiosity was combined with a robust good
nature that defied the hatred her point-
blank, thick-skinned *gaucherie* would otherwise have provoked. She watched the
unloading of a few van-loads of quite
new, but unpretending, furniture—" from
Maple's, my dear "—at the cottage with
the deepest interest, counting the number
of bedsteads—only four, and a child's cot
—which showed that Mrs. Hall did not
expect visitors—noting the style of the
arm-chairs and one sofa, the peculiarities
of the kitchen utensils, and such-like
apparently unimportant details with keen,
unwinking alertness.

The week after, when the small house

seemed to have subsided into order, she called. The tall, gaunt woman-servant, sallow, black-eyed, apparently approaching middle age, opened the door and confronted Miss Babb with a look of severe inquiry, which seemed to demand her ticket of admission. No severe looks ever penetrated Miss Babb's armour of self-confidence. She was the sort of person who needs to be knocked down by the butt end of a remonstrance.

"Your mistress in?" she inquired, producing a card. "I've called to see her."

"Yes, she's *in*," the woman answered, with uncompromising rectitude; "but she doesn't expect visitors."

"Oh!" Even while speaking Miss Babb was advancing step by step, as a soldier makes his way into a breach. "Well, you'll please to tell her I'm here, and give her my card."

The door which she had reached stood

open, and Miss Babb now confronted a hesitating and timid figure—that of the new owner of the cottage, who had neither the ready wit nor the nerve either to welcome or repel the determined invader. At the table, in a high chair, a large-eyed, serious-looking child, in a white pinafore, not far from the endearing baby stage— Miss Babb was fond of children—sat arranging some wooden animals in the vague yet strenuous fashion of chubby awkward little fingers. It was a handsome child on a large scale.

"Your little boy, ma'am?" Miss Babb said, diving at the small creature with an intention of kissing it, which the child frustrated by a quick turn of the head, which made the brim of Miss Babb's brown bonnet run into its eyes. It did not cry, however, only rubbed them hard.

"It's not a boy—it's a girl," faltered the mother, shyly. She spoke in a low, rather sweet-toned, but countrified voice. "She's called Penrose."

"Well, isn't that a boy's name? She don't look a bit like a girl, I declare. Well, ma'am, I thought I'd call. I'm your nearest neighbour, that's to say, except the poor folks at the corner of the lane, so I thought it but kind. I see you're settled in all right, and I dare say you'll find Copsley pleasant enough. On the whole it's a cheerful, neighbourly place, though we've all sorts. You can have as much visiting as you've a mind for."

"Oh, I—I've no mind for visiting, thank you," Mrs. Hall uttered, in tones of alarm almost bordering on terror. "I came here to be—to be quiet."

"Why?" doggedly inquired the unflinching Miss Babb. "You aren't a new-made widow. You don't wear weeds." She glanced at the plain black dress and the uncovered abundant locks.

"N—no; I—I don't."

Mrs. Hall apparently found nothing more sensible to say than this. Yet, Miss Babb reflected she surely *ought* to be in weeds, for the child could not be three.

"Your husband died when the little one was born ? How old is she ? "

" Two and a half."

"Where did you come from ? "

" From—from London."

Miss Babb persevered. She plied the new-comer with cut and thrust questions. She obtained vague, stupid, indefinite replies. She courted the boyish little girl with the large, clear, grey eyes and long up-curled eyelashes, and partly reconciled the latter to her presence, though Penrose still refused the demanded kiss, even seeming to prefer the hard brim of the bonnet. She got no more satisfaction from Mrs. Hall, and, leaving after half an hour, had reduced that poor woman almost to imbecility, and quite to tears.

She reported her interview to her great
ally, Mrs. Folliott, the vicar's wife, who
was new to Copsley herself, and zealous
to do the work of a new broom. Miss
Babb was evangelical in her views, and
differed essentially from Mrs. Folliott,
whose hobbies were Ritualistic services
and G.F.S. meetings, while the maiden
lady devoted herself to missionary boxes
and the manufacture of brown calico
pyjamas for the Africans ; but they forgot
their quarrels when neighbours had to be
discussed. Mrs. Folliott "thought it the
duty of the vicar's wife to be intimately
acquainted with the people in the parish."
Miss Babb "liked to be friendly with all
her neighbours." So on this unassailable
moral ground they met and discussed the
rest of their small world, over tea and hot
cakes at the Vicarage, or buttered toast at
Miss Babb's.

"Have you or the vicar called yet on
this lady at Heathside ? " was Miss Babb's

first question when she met the vicaress,
after the cottage was occupied that
Michaelmas twenty years ago.

"No; she hasn't been to church yet,"
Mrs. Folliott answered, with some gravity
—she put on an ecclesiastical air whenever she spoke of church. "I waited for
the Sunday to see. Did she go anywhere
else?"

The *anywhere else* was a sore point
to Mrs. Folliott. Copsley was a small
place, but it was, as she called it, "a
hotbed of Dissent." There was a
Wesleyan chapel as well as a Baptist,
flaunting their red-brick ugliness at the
grey old church, and the aristocratic
vicarage over the way. The best trades-
men in the town went to chapel, com-
pelling Mrs. Folliott to send to London
for her grocery and ironmongery; and the
church was never more than half filled.
The new surpliced choir, which made
naughty little corduroyed boys look like

young seraphs in their white robes, seemingly had no power of attraction to equal the loud singing of familiar old hymns, in which men, women, boys, and maidens could all join, and Mr. Folliott's brief, irreproachable sermonettes could not rival Mr. Lloyd's discourses at the Baptist chapel and Mr. Bates's at the Wesleyan.

"No," Miss Babb replied; "Mrs. Hall did not stir out all day; but the servant went to the Methodist place. She's a respectable-looking body. I wish I could get such a one; but as silent as her mistress. My Sarah can't get a thing out of her, but that they come from the south of England somewhere, and that Mrs. Hall lost her husband just after the child was born. It's rather a nice child; not shy, but quiet."

"Well, I shall wait and see if she goes to church. It doesn't seem as if this Mrs. Hall would be a great acquisition, anyhow."

And so, indeed, it had proved. Mrs. Hall was not a great acquisition. She made no mark in Copsley society. Miss Babb kept up a little casual acquaintance, and was kind on occasions, in her fussy, condescending way. No one had anything to say *against* her ; but, on the other hand, no one had much to urge *for* her, except a few destitute, beggarly, or disreputable folks, who did not count. She never turned any one from the door without a penny or a bit of food, was constantly and egregiously imposed upon, and had not anything hard to say of the laziest and least respectable ; but even with the poor she could not come out of her shell, which some called reserve and others stupidity. She was certainly not a brilliant woman ; all her movements were slow, heavy, lagging ; her voice, as well as her foot, faltered and halted. She never had anything to say to any one. She seemed to have no tastes, no strong opinions, no hatreds, no joys. She was always apparently placid and contented; yet through the mist of her invincible silence and reserve there was now and then something in her expression that told of a struggle, of suffering long gone by. She interested no one outside the cottage walls, and gave nothing to talk about, except that one reprehensible fact that she did not go to church. Whether it was active Dissent or apathy hardly appeared. Jane, her servant, went regularly every Sunday evening to the Wesleyan chapel, and once or twice her mistress and the little girl — who grew up to be a great girl almost unnoticed—went with her, but not regularly; and when Mr. Bates, the minister, called, Mrs. Hall was as chilly and unresponsive to him as to the vicar. She taught her child nothing of religion. She grew up entirely free to believe or not believe, except that Jane made her say the Lord's Prayer and a simple petition, such as children use, when she was little, and gave her an old-fashioned child's Bible, with frightful pictures in it, to read. Penrose soon grew to think the pictures hideous, and turned them over without a glance; but she loved to read the printed pages as she read everything, all the few story-books she possessed, and the small shelf full of queer, old-fashioned volumes, which it would have puzzled any one who knew anything of literature to find a reason for being collected by a person of education. Mrs. Hall seldom read. It was not her choice that had brought together that small library, which was a queerly assorted one enough. There was an old cookery-book, in which an illiterate hand had scrawled, " Eliz. Ames, her book, 1830," " Captain Cook's Voyage Round the World," Bunyan's " Pilgrim's Progress " and " Holy War," " Dr. Watts's Hymns," " Robinson Crusoe," some few volumes—some of them odd—evidently a lot from a second-hand bookstall, chiefly of adventure and discovery, a few modern mild story-books, " The Wide, Wide World," " The Lamp-lighter," " Uncle Tom's Cabin," and so on. In odd contrast to the rest, a prettily bound Tennyson and another illustrated gift-book or two were there also, which had the name " Mary " only written in them in a neat Oxford hand, and a date in the sixties.

Penrose had not much provision, it will be seen, to satisfy her craving for books ; but she knew all these nearly by heart, all except the cookery-book, and a very un-inviting volume of sermons.

When she was fifteen Mr. Folliott made a solemn professional call on her mother to ask if she were to be confirmed. Of course she was properly baptized ?

" Oh yes," Mrs. Hall said, in her nervous spasmodic way, feebly clasping her plump hands together, and colouring with the effort of speaking, "that was done quite right; I have the certificate."

"Then you will let her join my class, and be instructed for confirmation, of course," the vicar said blandly, but with firmness.

Mrs. Hall trembled and faltered, "Oh, I don't know, I'm sure, Penrose is very good. I don't know whether it is really necessary. I don't mind much either way—if she doesn't."

Mr. Folliott was shocked, yet baffled by the very ineptitude of the mother. To him it seemed terrible that she could speak as if such a thing were of little consequence either way, and refer it to the girl herself. Penrose came to church now pretty often in the evening, alone. She had been very attentive and thoughtful, but had somehow given the vicar the impression of a looker-on, more than as a young devotee.

"You'd better ask Pen herself," Mrs.

Hall went on, rising, as if gladly to escape any responsibility, or any further questioning. " I'll tell her to come."

" Is the woman wanting ? " the vicar asked himself, while he explained aloud with some warmth his views of a mother's duty in such a case, the wrong of neglect. But he could get nothing decisive from Mrs. Hall, she was not "brought up Church" herself, she said, she hardly knew what she was, she had not been confirmed ; but, if Pen wished it—and Pen seemed to like going to church—she should not object. Pen thought a deal about things, and wasn't like most girls of fifteen. She insisted on slipping out of the vicar's reach, and sending Penrose to him. It was just the way she always did. Penrose was the invariable receiver of everything that came their way that was difficult or disagreeable to manage, the shield placed between her mother and any perplexity, the referee in any dilemma. She had been thrust as a child into this position, reversing all the ordinary relations of mother and daughter. The vicar tried talking to her when she came as if she were any other village maiden in her teens, in a high, condescending tone of spiritual supremacy, as if she were immeasurably ignorant and childish ; yet, somehow, he was conscious of an odd difference in this greyeyed slip of a girl, who stood courageously, but not boldly before him in her plain short frock and holland apron, with a great thick plait of light brown hair hanging far below her waist like a ship's cable. Penrose was not a beautiful girl, but she was a striking one, and if not regularly pretty, had certain pronounced beauties. She promised to be tall, was upright and strong, though thin ; she had a very broad full forehead, not high, but intellectually made ; large, clear candid eyes, well opened, thickly fringed, meeting

the gaze with a sincere truthfulness that
could not possibly hide any subterfuge or
deceit; her well-shaped nose had delicate,
sensitive, proud nostrils ; her mouth was
not pretty, but it was full of character
and firmness, as was her square cleft chin.
Her complexion was of a clear, healthy
pale, slightly sunburnt, and not apt to
flush or change. She had a quantity of
hair, as I have said, springing strongly from
her forehead, with a large wave in it; it
grew more like a boy's than a girl's, and
there was something boyish altogether
in her face, bearing, and expression. She
had, it is true, never had a girl friend ; she
was not likely to have caught their ways,
even if it had been easy to her to assimilate,
which it most certainly was not. Mr..
Folliott was a man much narrowed by
aristocratic and sacerdotal prejudices, and
with a large mixture of the autocrat
about him ; but he was neither a stupid
nor an unkindly one, and his rather hard

eyes insensibly softened as they met the frank and simple truthfulness of the gaze which had nothing to hide from him.

"My dear," he said, in his hard, clear, metallic voice, " I want you to come to my class at the Vicarage, and be confirmed. Your mother is—has no objection."

"Very well," Penrose said quietly, " I shall not mind."

"Shall not mind! That is a strange way of speaking. You surely know what confirmation means ? "

" I think I do a little. I suppose I promise to be good and religious. I will try my best ; but, please may I go to chapel with mother if she wants me to ? I must. If being confirmed in church means that I am not— I cannot be. Mother is used to a chapel—if she goes anywhere—she likes it better than church ; she says the people stare at her so she gets confused."

The calm confidence of the child, which

was not rude or arrogant, confounded the lordly vicar. He waived the subject of the chapel, and proceeded to question the girl upon her faith. It was a self-taught one. Nobody but Jane had told her anything, and Jane was a Calvinist, whose views Penrose had instantly rejected with the positive directness of her nature. Left to herself and to the Bible, she had built up her own belief. The vicar thought it wanting in many respects in exact ortho-doxy, yet he could not find it in his heart to confute the happy confidence in God, in goodness, in the ideal life, in Christ, which somehow had grown out of the silent thoughts and the long solitary hours face to face with Nature which had formed this untutored girl. He could not help a sort of odd respect and admiration for her, and he left dogmatizing alone for the moment. Penrose was confirmed with the rest, in a simple white cotton frock and cap, like the poorer village girls.

Mr. Folliott had done what he could. He had to submit to seeing Penrose only occasionally at church, for, true to her word, she now and then accompanied her mother to the bare, barn-like edifice, with round-headed windows, where good old Mr. Bates, the unlearned but kindly natured Wesleyan minister, held forth. But Penrose meantime shot up into a maiden good to look upon, and of whom nobody, not even the most censorious and crabbed of a small and narrow world, could find anything worse to say than that she had "no manner," and was apt to be brusque where truth and politeness clashed. Yet, even where she had offended by this over sincerity, she was so honestly desirous to make friends, so ready to help, so constant and so unsparing of herself that resentment died, and she had no real enemies in Copsley.

A quieter, duller, more uneventful life could not be conceived. Penrose grew up to womanhood without having tasted gaiety, excitement, flirtation. She dressed and lived as plainly as an anchorite; she had no intimates, no gossiping girl confidantes to impart the more or less innocent nonsense which is the staple nourishment of most young minds. She got hold of hardly any novels, only a few old-fashioned ones of Miss Babb's, and some standard works which Mrs. Folliott recommended her. Her education was desultory in the extreme, even scanty, yet the soil was good, and the thinly scattered seed brought forth more abundantly than might have been expected. A mincing, affected little daily governess, the daughter of a farmer, who eked out her small resources by a little cheap teaching, used to come for a couple of hours in the morning during the years between ten and sixteen in Penrose's life. She imparted what knowledge she possessed in a fashion to make a high-school teacher shudder; so that Penrose learnt the dates of the kings and queens of England by heart, with all the worn-out old anecdotes and doubtful facts as inculcated by Mrs. Markham. She droned through " Cornwall's Geography," " Colenso's Arithmetic," and " Mangnall's Questions," learnt poetry from a book of selections, French to a *very* moderate extent, with a vile accent. Music was abandoned in despair. Penrose loved to listen, but her fingers had no flexibility; she had not an acute ear. Miss Finch gave this up. For drawing, however, the girl had a marked talent, and she was here more fortunate in an instructor.

In the village lived an old artist, a man who had never been successful, yet who had something of a wayward genius in him. He took a fancy to Penrose Hall when she was a little wandering maid, following her own sweet will in rambling unprotected on common or in copse, and who stood spellbound by the hour to watch him. He was drawn at last by her mute admiration and un-exacting companionship to offer to teach her how to paint. He provided her with materials, and set her tasks which were pastimes. She was perfectly happy with a pencil or brush for long hours. They were fast friends and comrades, though but little talk passed between them. This quiet-spoken, almost boorish elderly man, and one or two of the poorer village folks, were Penrose's only real friends outside the walls of Heathside Cottage. At the time of which I now speak she was in her twenty-third year, and they had been at Copsley nearly twenty years without variation of its monotonous routine.

No girl had lived a quieter and more secluded life.

Mrs. Hall seldom cared to go a mile from home, and, with the exception of four visits a year to London, whither Jane accompanied her till Penrose grew old

enough to be her protector, she scarcely
ever made even a short journey.

These quarterly pilgrimages exercised
Miss Babb's mind, for she had always a
restless sense that there was " something
odd " about her quiet neighbour, and she
vainly tried to extract information about
herself from the reticent, silent, shy woman,
whose blank irresponsiveness often irritated
the small eager mind of the spinster lady.
It was to " fetch her dividends," Mrs. Hall
replied to a point-blank question as to
these London errands, and no more could
be got at, not even where they were paid
nor the amount. But she never seemed
poor. They spent little at the cottage,
because no one cared to spend ; but Mrs.
Hall paid ready money for everything,
never grumbled at prices, and was "foolishly
lavish," as Miss Babb considered, in charities
and subscriptions. Mystery or no mystery,
the widow was absolutely impenetrable as
to her past ; she seemed to have hardly

any opinions, and she had no fund of con-
versation at all. Copsley had grown used
to her not unhandsome, though time-
worn face, her heavy creeping movements,
low hesitating voice, and soft timid eyes.
No one disliked, but no one actively cared
for her outside the small circle of her
home, and she seemed to crave no affection,
no notice, and to be content with the
narrow range and dull tranquillity which
cramped her life within such meagre
limits. Even Miss Babb only occasionally
wondered what the early habits had been
which landed her in this seclusion.

CHAPTER VII.

"JANE, I'm often frightened when I think of Penrose."

These words broke a long silence, and continued a disjointed, but not emotionless talk which Mrs. Hall had been carrying on in the neat kitchen of Heathside Cottage. Quiet as she was Mrs. Hall never cared to be left entirely alone ; to be without any companion but her own slow-passing thoughts seemed always to make her nervous, and when her daughter was out she generally took her knitting and sat in the kitchen, or else helped Jane in her work in a vague, indolent kind of way. Jane was not a common-looking person, she had a decided individuality.

Thirty years ago, or even less, she must have been a handsome woman in a rather masculine way. Her hair, iron-grey now, would have been beautiful when it was black, she twisted it up into as hard and small a knot as she could now; but it was still thick and crisp, and contrasted with her very dark eyebrows and brown skin which, though wrinkled, was wholesome, clean and agreeable still to look at. Her steady dark eyes could be fierce when she frowned and pursed up her thin lips; but there were times when a kind, beneficent gleam lightened them and they were always honest and true. She was tall and straight as a poplar, neat, quick, and strong in all her movements—tender over babies and animals. Her manner with her mistress was one of perfect calm equality, in fact rather authoritative than otherwise, and Mrs. Hall never dreamt of disputing her will. She could be passionate and rude, but with one person she was at times yielding. This was Penrose, she acknowledged a mistress in her only. Yet Penrose was always gentle in her manner to Jane.

The kitchen was cleaned up, shining with scrubbing and polishing on this Saturday afternoon, when Jane generally finished her labours by rubbing the small supply of silver, and all the shining brasses and tins which the household boasted. The fire burnt with a steady glow, pleasant to every sense as the spring twilight crept in. The wood of the table and dresser was white as the freshly stoned hearth. Mrs. Hall sat in an elbow-chair, rather spasmodically rubbing a few teaspoons with a leather, while Jane put her usual vigour into the polishing of some candle-sticks from the shelf.

"What d'ye mean?" she asked, in her trenchant abrupt tones. Nature had given her a fine contralto voice, which might have been a beautiful organ had not Jane always spoken abruptly, with a smack of some rustic accent. "Frightened when you think of Penrose? Why?"

"If ever she got to know things," Mrs. Hall hesitated out in her faltering way, "I think I couldn't bear it very well."

"There's no reason she ever should. And if she *did*——"

"Oh, hush, Jane!"

"Well, if she did, you're her mother, and she loves you. She ain't a girl to turn on any one. You know that well enough."

"I know; but I couldn't bear she'd have to, Jane. I wonder and wonder however Pen comes to be what she is. She's not a bit like me, not in one single thing."

"No, only that she's got a soft heart over children and beasts, and don't like to see folks suffer."

"Only in that. She couldn't else be

more different; and she's not like—not at all like her—her father."

" No."

A pause of silent rubbing, which Jane broke.

" You're right. She's not a mite like you, not what you are nor what you was, not a mite. But there's freaks of that kind everywhere, folks come odd in families just as carrots and parsnips do at whiles. Why now, *you* were an odd one. Who did you take after? Not your mother nor father, nor any of 'em. Maybe, Penrose is like one as is dead and gone, or else the Lord made her fresh after a pattern of his own."

" She ought to have been a boy, I think sometimes, so strong and fearless as she is; never would tell a lie, not to save herself any pain, and would face anything, now wouldn't she?"

Jane nodded. " Ay, that she would. And you just as scared as you can be at every mortal thing, if a mouse squeaks, or a dog jumps on you, or there's a winding-sheet in the candle. No. I never knew a more fearless creature than she be, nor a more fearsome one than you."

"You remember her mastering that drunken gipsy?"

Jane nodded again.

"I always feel when she's by, as if I couldn't be afraid. I sleep at night now, as if there was a man in the place. It often makes me wonder to see her. But all the more it terrifies me when I get thinking that some day she'll know it all, maybe, and turn against me." The feeble voice began to quiver, the full double chin showed symptoms of a climbing sob.

"That's stuff," Jane said roughly, though her eyes had their kinder look. "I say she ain't one of that sort. Once care is always care with her. She's not the girl to turn against her mammy. And the

Lord knows you've been a fond mother to her."

"Why, of course I've been! What else have I had but the child? And the dearest little thing as she was, with her queer masterful ways, yet as loving with them all. 'You're tired, mothie,' she'd say, when she was but a bit of a thing, so high—'you look tired—just lie down and I'll cuddle you.' I used to think she must be a changeling left by the angels, she was so much better than I ever thought she could be!"

A few large, easy tears rolled down the pale cheeks of the mother. Tears came to her with as little trouble and pain, as smiles do to some natures; they hardly reddened her eyelids, and she wiped them away with simple unconsciousness. With the two people who were her only intimates in all the world, Mrs. Hall lost her stolid, blank, undeviating reserve, and had no shame at showing her emotions.

Jane, who was of sterner stuff, and had only shed a few secret tears in all her life, was a little impatient.

"What are you crying for?" she asked, setting down her bright candlestick with emphasis. "You've got a comfortable home as suits you, and the best of daughters, healthy and happy—there's nought to fret about."

"No, only I wonder at times what I'd do if she thought ill of me."

"Don't, then. Don't be fancying things. You have been talking this way since you went to London. What was it set you off? Anything as that lawyer fellow said? You've not been your own self since, and you might as well tell me the reason of it. You know when you keep a thing to yourself it frets and troubles you till you get it out, and it's a good thing for you as you've got me to tell it to."

"He did upset me a bit, Jane; but

I don't know exactly what he meant. He's an odd, baffling way with him. You know I see him alone most times, he hardly ever asks for Pen, but this time he did. He and I were alone at first, and after he'd paid me, he stared at me in that secret sort of knowing way he has, and said something. I was fluttered, and could not rightly say what the words were, something about changes that might come, but not changes to hurt. Then he asked to see Pen, and he eyed her all over. She stood just as she does, so upright, and not a bit scared, and looked back at him. And he smiled, and said she'd grown into a fine woman all at once, and that he was sure she must be my right hand—both my hands, he might have said ;—that was all, there was nothing to take hold of, but just that word ' change.' Jane, the word itself frightens me ! I shiver to think of any change."

" Why, there must be," Jane cried, " it's

a world of change! You can't reckon on things going on like this humdrum, humdrum for ever! You and me must get old and die "—Mrs. Hall shuddered. "Ay, I know you dread it, poor soul; but it must be, soon or late. Then there's Penrose growed, as he says, into a woman, and a fine, fair, wholesome woman too, some one might come to love her."

"There's no one here," Mrs. Hall cried eagerly, raising her white, clumsily shaped, soft hands with a gesture as if she would push away some unwelcome intruder. "Pen doesn't think of such things, it isn't her way."

"Not her way! Now don't be selfish— she's a woman. Why shouldn't it come her way to find out a woman's lot. She can't always be looking after you, and caring for you, as if you were the child and she the mother. Don't you stand in her light now, whatever happens."

"Oh, but I hope nothing will happen!"

the mother cried, almost in a wail. " It's best to go on just as we do, and Pen's happy enough, you know she is, Jane!"

"Happy enough! I'd like to know what most girls 'ud think of that *enough*," Jane returned in an angry voice. "What suits you isn't going to suit her for ever. You only want to be quiet and peaceful, and for no one to stir up a thought about what's past and gone ; but there's all her future for Pen to think about, to be made good or bad for her, and it ain't to be expected as this sort of little half-asleep living can do for any one like her for ever and a day. Look what other girls want, look what other girls have! Why, even here, in this little dull hole of a place, look at the misses at the vicarage, at the doctor's, at the big farmhouse over yonder. Look at their smart clothes, their junketings and picnics, their dancing and playing of games, their young fellows, and all the rest of it. And there's our

Penrose, with her one common gown and her best—no ribbons nor fal-lals, no one saying nice things to her—though she'd beat any of 'em in looks—no play or fun. I tell you it didn't ought to be, and if change to you meant a change for the better for her, you'd be a bad mother to oppose it."

"I've never meant to be a bad mother, God knows, Jane," the other faltered out. More tears might have followed had not the quick opening and shutting of the front door sounded at the moment, and Penrose's eager, firm step.

She threw open the kitchen door when she found the parlour empty and dark. Excitement flushed her cheek which only grew rosy under strong feeling, and her large clear eyes shone bright. It was, however, a painful emotion, the lines of her mouth and the contraction of her forehead showed this.

"Mother dear," she said, in a voice

which she kept calm by a strong effort
of repression, usual to her when dealing
with her easily scared mother, " I want
to know if you'll let me bring Lucy
Evans in here for to-night, at any rate.
I found her under the hedge, ill—very
ill, I'm afraid. They'd turned her away
from her father's cottage. I don't know
who would take her in, and I can't let
her die out there."

" Lucy Evans ! The girl who—the girl
who——" a gathering remembrance of the
circumstances made Mrs. Hall suddenly
colour and tremble.

" The girl that was in service to Morton,
and went wrong," Jane put in uncom-
promisingly.

" Yes," Penrose said quickly, as if the
words stung her. " I know all about
that now ; Lucy told me. Her mistress
sent her away, and she's very ill, in dreadful pain, cold, starved, and miserable. She
was trying to get to the workhouse, but

it's terrible in there; they are so hard to the girls, and her own father and mother are the hardest of all. Mother, I'll look after her, and nurse her, if you won't mind. We can't leave her, and go by on the other side."

"Where is she?" said the faint, stammering voice, out of the half darkness. "Not outside now?"

"No, in the passage. I was only waiting to take her upstairs. I may, mayn't I? I know I may."

"Yes, dear, what you will; only——" She broke off and touched Jane imploringly. "Jane, *you'll* see to her—not Pen."

Jane said not a word; she put down what was in her hands, wiped them on her apron, and went to the door.

"I'll see the girl to bed, Penrose," she said abruptly, as she reached it. "Do you just air some things, and then, when she's all right, I'll go to Dr. Bentley's.

'Tain't fit for you, at your age, to be doing such jobs."

" That's nonsense, Jane," Penrose said calmly, smiling as she spoke; "as if I hadn't been used to all sorts of things in the village; as if I wasn't grown up! I can do anything Lucy wants."

"You'll not, then, I tell you," Jane returned, with sudden severity; "your mother don't wish you to. I'll see to the wench myself. I'm not for turning her adrift, or for being cruel; but I've little doubt she's none fit for you to be with."

Penrose was reluctant to give way. She trusted Jane's real goodness, but feared its harshness of expression, and her heart yearned over the desolate outcast she had brought home. But Jane was inexorable. Penrose might only help in bringing what was wanted in preparing food, and waiting on her mother in the absence of the one servant; she

must not come in to comfort the girl with
her ungrudging tenderness. And her
mother, too, kind as she always was to
the poor and ill, oddly enough seemed
also to hate her being with Lucy, and
kept her by her own side with feeble
insistence. She shrank from talking of
the suffering girl. Oh yes, anything
might be done for her while she was too
ill to be moved! She did not grudge
anything; but she would not see Doctor
Bentley — would hardly let Penrose tell
her what was the matter, nor how dangerous the girl's state was. Jane kept the
door shut on her, and her mother clung
to her presence. Penrose was not satisfied
to stand aloof; but, though strong, she
was not stubborn, and she yielded, not
because she understood, but because her
mother had set her heart on it. Only
she rejoiced to know, as the rain suddenly
came crashing on the roof, and pelting
like a mad thing against their windows,

with a howling gusty wind in pursuit of
it, that the forlorn girl was safely housed,
and, whatever came to her now, at least
she had human care and help about her,
and was not left to bear the agony and
the desolation alone in the cruel and
bitter storm, that is no crueller than Fate
to such wrecks of humanity as the wickedness of the world has created. Her mother
was odd about this, turning the subject
persistently from the girl upstairs—odd,
and even unusually nervous in manner.
But Penrose was accustomed to these
little eccentricities. Much as she shared
with her, dearly as she loved her, always
as they were together, she had found out
before she grew up that, simple, even
shallow as that mother seemed in some
ways, there were depths in her which she
had never penetrated, a silence which met
her blankly now and then like a dividing
wall she could not pass, a baffling though
soft resistance which she could no more

overcome than a shot can penetrate a feather-bed. But in spite of this passive holding back, and Jane's more active resolution that she should not be with Lucy, Penrose could not be kept from her share of ministering; for the girl grew rapidly worse—the cold and exposure, the misery of mind and body telling on an exhausted frame, brought on acute inflammation of the lungs and pleurisy, with no remnant of strength to resist them. She cried out for the young lady with half-delirious obstinacy, and Jane had no heart to refuse. Penrose had gone to bed, but was not asleep, in her little room opening out of her mother's, when Jane entered, tall, grey, and gaunt in her night *déshabillé*.

"Penrose," she said, in a subdued voice, "it's no use giving way to your mother's wish about this; you must come along and see if you can quiet that poor dying wench. She is a-dying; I'm well enough used to

sickness to see the look on her face there's
no mistaking, and she calls and calls for
you. I'm a Christian woman, and I can't
refuse her any comfort, if comfort it be.
She's dying—hurried into her grave by
bad, black-hearted folks ; and maybe the
Lord 'll reckon in what she's bearing now
against the day of judgment. Come along
to her. Your mother's asleep ; we needn't
worrit her, poor soul."

Penrose had leapt out of bed, and hurried
on her dressing-gown before the first words
were well out of Jane's lips. Her long
thick hair hung in one great cable down
her back, her firm young face was set
into an expression of pain sternly held
back from emotion. She looked like a
picture of some early martyr, or like the
angel with the sword, so blended in her
face was deep, strong, intense compassion
and self-control. In another minute she
was bending over Lucy, whose wild, burning eyes turned to hers with imploring

anguish in their brown depths, and whose
fluttering, dry, hot hands caught hold of
hers.   Jane was right ; it was Death that
had sharpened the thin features of the once
pretty, careless face, and hollowed the
temples and eye-sockets with the touch
of his fingers.   Her breath came short,
rattling, distressed, broken by a dry, weak
cough, which racked without relieving the
wasted, quivering body.

"Oh, Miss Hall, you was always good
to me—you gave me flowers and apples
out of the garden when you and me was
little girls together ; you was sorry for me
out there in the rain, when father shut the
door on me.   You'll be sorry for me now ?
you'll try and help me, won't you ? though
I'm a bad girl—a bad girl, and you be
good.   Miss Hall, you'll be kind to me ?
I'm so ill—I'm so ill !   You'll be a bit
sorry for me, won't you, though I'm bad ? "

Penrose stroked the rough hair, and
pressed the poor head to her breast.   Her

heart seemed breaking with pity; she wanted to be omnipotent for the moment, to give Lucy help and solace. Her strong, brave, tender soul was all one throb of pity. But words are so weak, and as for deeds—— Dear God, what can we do, in the chains of our mortal limitations, when Thine unhappy little ones call upon us to help them?

"Lucy, Lucy dear, I wish I could take the suffering away! I wish I could help you through! I'd bear it for you if I could. Poor girl! poor Lucy! Is there anything I can do?"

"Yes, yes, only hold me—hold me. You're so kind; you're so sorry for me. Jane's been praying to God for me. Jane's kind, too; but I know she thinks I'm lost, and haven't got a chance to be forgiven. You pray, too, for you don't think I'm as bad as she does; and you and me was little girls together."

Penrose held the poor head to her

strongly, yet softly, half sitting, half kneel-
ing, and murmured words of entreaty to
God for pity, mixed with the tenderest
broken assurances of her own love.

Jane stood silent and still, her strong
hard face scarcely relaxed; yet in her
heart there was pity for the dying girl,
and deep, deep affection for the other.
She left all ministrations to her. She did
not try any longer to pray or to exhort.
It suddenly came upon her that this God
to whom Penrose's heart was crying was
not the God she had thought she knew,
not the stern Judge who hardly might
pardon sin, even when sin melted into a
very fountain of tears, but the Father
who had made such children possible,
who had inspired such a great heart as
this girl had, who would have given her
own strength and safety, her own freedom
from pain and woe gladly for the waif and
outcast from her own home who had fallen
broken-hearted at their threshold. It

seemed as if some power not her own
had entered into Penrose and given her
a miraculous healing to the bruised
trembling spirit just lingering on the
solemn twilight verge. Lucy's cries ceased.
She lay still, exhausted, but with a sort
of peace upon her, infinitely mournful, yet
no longer terrible to look at. Her young,
drawn, altered face grew greyer, more and
more solemn, less and less like the girl
the village knew and scorned, lying quietly
on Penrose's warm and tender breast.
A few broken, whispering words came
sobbing out of her pale lips now and then.
" God bless you ! you've been so good.
I'm not frightened now. Don't you go
away and leave me. I'm sorry—sorry—
sorry."

At last Penrose's great eyes gathered
slow tears, which fell one by one on the
girl's rough light hair. The faint clinging
of the dying hands on hers would not
relax to let her wipe them off; but they

were the very dew of mercy, and blessed the living and the dying.

Jane held aloof, not in harshness, but in a curious reverence, feeling that she had no part here. Only at last she came gently forward to lay back the lifeless head and press a kind hand on the half open eyelids. Then she kissed Penrose suddenly; she had not done so for many a year.

"The Lord bless and keep thee, dear," she said. "You've a merciful heart. There's no fear that you'll judge them as have sinned; the Lord has put His love into you."

Mrs. Hall woke next morning with a start to find Jane standing by her with a curious grave look, softer than its wont, on her strongly cut features.

"That poor thing's dead," she said; "and I do believe the Lord has took her to a better home than she's ever had a chance of."

"Dead, Jane; here, in this house? Oh, Jane!"

"Well, we can't live outside of death altogether," Jane returned almost sternly. "It's well as she come here, anyway. It's been made as easy to her as it could be, thanks to that blessed girl of yours. Neither you nor me have ever known all there is in Penrose, I tell you. You needn't ever be afeared of *her* being hard. Somehow or other she's got a heart of gold, and you ought to thank the Lord every day of your life that she's your own, and loves you. I never knew what she had about her till last night, though I always loved her. I tell you Penrose is one in a thousand, and the good Lord is bound to reward her for her loving-kindness to that poor sinful thing that's gone out of life in a moment. I humoured you to keep her away all I could; but I've a heart for others beside you, and I couldn't refuse her when she cried

and cried for her. I'm glad to my very
heart as I didn't. I tell you I shall
never forget this last night to my dying
day. It's made a difference to me that
I shan't get over. Now, don't you fret
or moan over what's happened, and what's
got to be done. The girl's dead, and
there's an end of it, and you must face it.
You shan't have more worry over it, you
may depend, than Penrose and me can
prevent. And you shan't see her, for I
know it makes you bad, poor soul, for you
never could abide the thought or sight of
death."

CHAPTER VIII.

THE episode of Lucy Evans' death passed away as even terrible episodes pass, leaving no visible trace, yet it was not without some effects. It deepened Jane's feeling for Penrose, which had always been strong though silent. It gave Penrose new thoughts, and an intense pity for suffering, a stronger desire to help. It made the neighbours wonder at, yet condescend to admire, the kindness of the people at the Cottage. It stirred a passing remorse and shame in the coarse, cruel folks, who had been less than kind to the outcast of their own kin. But especially Penrose's mother pondered and brooded over what she never spoke of and tried to put away. She was a woman of a curiously tenacious memory; she had had but few events and fewer changes in her life. For twenty years she had vegetated in one quiet spot, leading a harmless, apparently absolutely peaceful existence, with nothing visibly to disturb or unsettle her. All the more vivid, therefore, remained the few strongly marked memories of her youth. Not a day passed but her mind slowly revolved the visions which had never grown dim, misty, or far away, though a long gulf of years lay between them and the apathetic calm of the present. Outwardly she droned through the little affairs of an unbroken routine, looked after her garden, dawdled on the common, did a little languid work, knitted or sewed, ate and slept soundly. A "poor good creature," the neighbours called her, "with nothing much in her and heavy to get on with." But her inward life went on side by side with this tranquil monotony, with its secrets, its possessions, its aches and inarticulate craving, and not a soul knew one syllable of the sealed volume, or at least but one, and she only guessed, and often guessed wrong. The awful solitudes of even bare, meagre souls are always impressive. It is a frightening thought to dwell on, that we all inhabit, each absolutely alone, a desert island set in the " unplumbed, salt, estranging sea."

The one disturbing, most disturbing, thought that rose again and again in this silence of her own heart whenever she began to revolve her daily memories, was that suggestive word " change," which the lawyer had thrown out in their last interview. " Change " she dreaded, shrank from it, yet she felt it in the air, she looked out for it, trembling. What could he have meant ? And what change could there be that would not confound and shake her into terror ? She did not often pray with any reality, though, out of habit, she repeated nightly a mechanical form. The great event of her life had shaken to pieces the old ignorant faith of her girlhood, and she had never had power enough to put the broken bits coherently together. But one prayer rose again and again with an obstinate yet hopeless desire, that nothing might disturb the life to which her timid soul had grown used, that she might not have to find out any new way of existence, but be left in the half peace which was her substitute for happiness. She hated innovations, even of the smallest kind. Any alteration in the mode of living into which she had somehow shaken, frightened and upset her.

Jane and Penrose—the only people who had any real influence on her mind—were careful to save and spare her, tacitly agreed on a kind of indulgent petting which neither ever defined or sought any reason for.

"Your mother likes this; your mother wants that." These phrases were enough to make Penrose give up ungrudgingly, even when her mother's wishes came in the way, all the relaxations and pursuits which she might have found for herself even in dull little Copsley, if it had been possible to her to put her own desires first. She had longings, like other girls; she wanted, as all ardent young people must, to stretch her cramped wings and take a flight into freedom. She felt, though without openly complaining of them, the hampering limits of her straitened life. Her old artist friend urged her to make a real pursuit of art. She had enough in her, he said, if she gave her time to it, to make something as satisfactory of it in a small way as other smaller painters. As it was she let everything interfere, and could not get beyond the amateurish. Penrose always shook her head sadly enough, and answered briefly that nothing more was possible to her. At every turn, when she tried to move in any direction, those invisible threads held her which her mother had woven round her like the witch Maimuna. If she strained, and tried to break them, they would pull on that mother's heart and hurt her. *She* must have what she wanted, whatever Penrose went without. So it was that Penrose had no girl friends. She would have liked to know what people of her own age thought and felt. She had sometimes a wish to throw off the gravity which had got to be a habit, and be merry, to laugh at nothing, and "frivol" a little with the rest. But "mother did not like to have people in," and naturally no one went out of their way to run after Penrose, who had nothing to offer in return. Mrs. Folliott had asked her to working parties at the Vicarage, and was condescendingly kind in her bland aristocratic way when it struck her; but the

working parties were not lively. A dull
book was read aloud in a high monotone
by the vicar, who could not help intoning
even in private life, and the girls who were
intimate gossiped in whispers. Celia and
Grace Folliott, rather pretty, flirty, proud
girls, did not unbend to Penrose Hall,
who was dressed as plainly as a nun, had
no small-talk, and was not "in society,"
in short, at all, though no one ever
ventured to call her *common*—no one could
do that. One glance at her clear-cut
noble face was enough, and her sincere
rich contralto voice had a refinement in
every accent that the most casual hearer
could not miss. No, she was not vulgar,
only just not get-on-able-with ; not used
to the society shibboleth, the everyday
topics of ordinary young ladies. There
was nothing to go upon with her, and the
other girls were just civil, and no more.
The half-proud, half-pathetic look in her
clear grey eyes did not appeal to rather

ordinary minds such as these were. So, after a while, Penrose left off coming to the working parties, partly because of the feeling of loneliness she could not fight off altogether, partly because her mother passively opposed them, not openly giving any objection, but hinting and hindering in her vague hesitating way.

Now and then Penrose drank tea with Miss Babb, and did little services for her. The garrulous, active, managing old lady, with all her faults of unbridled gossiping and absolute density of the finer feelings, was good-natured enough, and had a neighbourly liking for the cottage people, though she still maintained that there was "something odd" about Mrs. Hall's secretiveness. She took an interest in most people, though not always a friendly one; and Penrose sometimes found it a relief to sit an hour or two in the prim old-fashioned little sitting-room, full of the carefully preserved relics of a very unæsthetic youth—terribly painted hand-screens, worsted-work stools, bead cushions, and the like ; to chat or to read some novel aloud, with a running comment from Miss Babb, who liked the sound of her own voice, and believed in her own critical powers to an amusing extent. It was provoking to the old lady that she never could succeed in pumping her girl visitor ; and, either because she had inherited her mother's reserve, or because she knew nothing, had no interesting bits of information to give about that voiceless past of her mother's which had always puzzled and baffled Miss Babb's inquiring mind. To be sure she had found out that the quarterly visits to town were paid to a solicitor called Hamley in Gray's Inn, but that was not much to go upon. Penrose believed he was her mother's trustee. Beyond this Miss Babb could not get. Penrose did not even know the amount of her mother's income. Apparently they had not a relation in the world—at any rate, Penrose knew of neither uncle, aunt, nor cousin ; her mother's parents, she had been told, were dead. Their name had been Chegwidden ; her grandmother's maiden name was in the old cookery book, "Elizabeth Ames." She believed her grandfather had been a sea captain— her mother often spoke of him with affection. Her mother she had not loved so much ; she was a hard woman, she often said. These few meagre facts were all that Miss Babb had ever gleaned from Penrose, and she could only supplement them by her imagination.

"Chegwidden ! That's a Cornish name, I know ; and, to be sure, so, I suppose, that odd name of yours is—Penrose ! I've often wondered at it. Tre, Pol, and Pen, they're all Cornish. D'ye know, child, where your mother lived before she was married ? "

" No ; but I believe it was in the south or west."

"Cornwall, no doubt. Well, that's something to know. It's odd, isn't it, that you've no relations?"

"Very odd," said Penrose calmly; and somehow, as she looked straight at the old lady with those honest eyes of hers that had nothing to hide and no shame to conceal, Miss Babb let her researches drop.

It happened, fortunately for Mrs. Hall, as it turned out, that Penrose was spending the evening in this way with Miss Babb when the postman called at Heathside Cottage and left a thick letter. It was very seldom letters came, or anything but a tradesman's circular, to the house, and Mrs. Hall trembled all over as Jane silently put it in her hand, and stood by, as if waiting for news.

Mrs. Hall looked at it first vaguely, then with a growing disturbance, shrinking from opening it, as it was her habit to shrink from any new thing that might hide a terror.

"It's from Mr. Hamley, I believe," she said faintly.

"Open it and see," Jane returned, in her strong voice, regardless of the tremor that she was apt to scorn. "Where's the sense of staring at the outside like that? What can harm you in a letter from Mr. Hamley?"

"I — I don't know; but I'm afraid, Jane!"

"Pooh! don't be so skeary, woman! Open it, or give it me."

Mrs. Hall slowly tore open the envelope, as if she suspected it contained an explosive, slowly read it, and uttered a cry. There was an enclosure in a cramped, curious hand.

"What is it? Can't you speak?" Jane asked, fiercely impatient. "What does the man say? Who's the other from?"

"Read it. Oh dear, oh dear! I was afraid there was some change coming— something to upset me. Read it—can

you ?—aloud. There's such a mist, I can't
be sure of what he does say ; and I am so
frightened. Read it, Jane."

"If I can," Jane said doubtfully ; "but
it's none so easy."

She spelled out slowly word by word,
while Mrs. Hall sat upright, white and
shaking, with the other letter clutched
tightly between her hands—

"DEAR MADAM,

"Mr. Trevenna has asked me to forward
enclosed. Therein you will see the proposition he
makes to you, which you will allow me, in your own
interests and in that of your daughter, to urge you to
accept without delay. If you do so, I will take all
trouble of arrangement off your hands, and make
every preparation for your stay in town. I should
advise your coming thither early next week, and will,
if you permit, engage nice quiet rooms for you near
my chambers. Every detail shall be carefully studied
for your comfort, with a view to sparing you any
disagreeables.

"Yours faithfully,

"THOMAS HAMLEY."

"Well, that's all French till we see
what the other one says," Jane said, when

she had laboured through the short note with some difficulty. " He seems to write very civil ; but I don't know what he means. Don't be foolish, now ; open it quick, and let us get this over as soon as may be."

" I feel as if I couldn't, Jane."

" Shall I ? Will you give it me, Mary ? " The servant woman had seated herself beside the other. She put her large, brown, capable hand on her shoulder with an air of protection ; her voice had grown gentle. But the weak, trembling fingers kept their grasp of this other letter. A sort of shudder and sob ran through her.

" No ; I will in a minute, Jane. I haven't had a letter from *him* for twenty years ! "

" More shame to him," muttered the other, in a harsh guttural voice.

" I'm afraid what he may say. I shouldn't have known the handwriting,

Jane; it's all altered. Mr. Hamley said he'd been very ill."

"He's no young man. Don't work yourself up over it, now; it ain't worth while your grieving. It's over, Mary, over and dead like last year's leaves. Read it; maybe it's nought but a bit of law business. There's no likelihood of more than that betwixt you two."

Still shuddering a little, as if with cold, Mrs. Hall opened the enclosure. She did not this time give it to Jane to read, her eyes slowly followed the crabbed lines, written with fingers cramped with pain; and then she folded it up, and sat without a word, as if she were turned to stone by the terrifying surprise of what she had slowly made out.

"Come, tell me what he says," Jane cried, angry with the silence, shaking the shoulder slightly, on which her hand rested.

"Don't," the other moaned; "let me think—let me be quiet."

Another minute passed, and then she began to falter out a word, suddenly checked, as she started up; then seized her letters, and hurried to the door.

"Hush, hush! That's Pen at the garden gate; I can't see her! Jane, I'm going to bed. Tell her my—my head aches; she's not to come in to me. Get her her supper, and, when she's busy, come, and I'll tell you what it is; but I can't see Pen. Mind you don't let her in my room."

She hastened stealthily upstairs, and Jane, after her wont, with an inward protest, carried out her wishes.

CHAPTER IX.

THIS was the letter which Mrs. Hall
had read. It began abruptly—

"I have been for some time much occupied in
thought over the past, and our former relations together. I treated you badly, I spoilt your life, and
you have every reason to hate me. I am very ill now,
and not likely to last long, and I think I should be
glad to set things as far right as is possible after a
life of wrong. If you are willing, I will give you the
name and position of my wife. Hamley will arrange
all details with you. After my death you would have
my property, and the girl after you. I am aware it
is a very unsatisfactory atonement at the best; but I
think you will gain more than you lose. You need
not write to me, I should prefer all communications
passing through Hamley; if you agree, just notify the
same to him, and I will meet you in town the day you
fix. I will endeavour to spare you throughout as
much as I can.

"Yours, etc.,
"RICHARD TREVENNA."

While Penrose was at her simple supper, with a book beside her, Jane stole upstairs into the darkened room, where Mrs. Hall lay, clutching the letter in one hand, the other on her heart, which beat audibly in heavy thuds under it, her face was turned to the wall. The servant —if she can be thus called—sat down on the bed, and put her hand, with an anxious solicitude that was as nearly tender as her manner permitted, on the burning forehead.

"I expect your head do ache truly enough," she said. " How it throbs ; and your poor heart, too ! Come, Mary, take courage ; tell me what there is in that letter to make you in this twitter. But, poor soul, you never had a mite of spirit ! Now tell us — it'll ease you."

Mrs. Hall turned towards her, so that her whispering voice should reach the ear bent down to her.

" Jane, I feel as if—I don't know how I feel—stunned, dazed like. I'm not sure

I'm awake; it's knocked me over. He wants—he asks—he says——" Her voice failed, and broke altogether.

"There now, there!" the other said, as if she were soothing a child in a nightmare. "Try and get quiet; there can't be nothing to scare you so. Why should you trouble about what he's got to say to you? You're not a girl now; he can't get a hold of your life any more."

"Jane, he says he'll marry me!" The words were jerked out with a kind of spasm, and she caught hold of the firm bony arm that was near her, and clung to it as for support.

"Marry you!" Strong astonishment was in the two words. "And what for—*now*, Mary? It's years too late for the likes of that!"

"He's ill, not going to live long; he says it's to make amends." The words were barely audible.

"Make amends!" Jane gave a short

laugh, harsh as a saw. "Amends to a woman for over twenty years' shame! That's a good notion."

"Hush. He says he knows he spoilt my life ; but, after all, I won't be sure of that. I've not been so miserable. I think I'd be no better off married, Jane. I think I'll say things shall stay as they are." The low, faltering words were hesitated out as if she felt they had no force, and knew what her listener would say.

"What does he want to do it for ? " Jane asked sternly, with abrupt directness.

"He would leave me his property, and Penrose after me—I'd take his name. But we are very comfortable—we don't want more money, do we ? I'd better not change."

"Don't be a fool," the other returned almost fiercely ; "you've got to do it, whether you like or no. It's late in the day, God knows. There's no putting things straight after what's come and gone ; but

to die an honest woman, with a right to
your wedded name, and to leave the girl
well off—you've *got* to do it, Mary! I've
stuck to you and fended you; but I've
never called wrong right, or blame praise.
I never thought to live to see you in the
place you'd ought to have had then. I
say you *shall* marry him. Why, think
of this—if you think of nothing else—
suppose the man died without making
provision for you and her, where'd you
be then? How'd you get on without a
home or a shilling? If 'twas me I'd make
a living anywhere; but you—you couldn't
do nothing now to earn a crust. I say
you must do this, and thank the Lord for
giving you the chance."

"But, Jane," the frightened, quivering
voice wailed out, "I can't bear to go
through with it—to see him again, after
twenty years, and meet him so—to stand
and be married—me with my grey hair—
me with my grown girl. Jane, I can't—
I can't have Pen know."

"'Can't,' 'can't,' always 'can't' this and that!" the woman cried, starting impatiently away from the clutching hands, and almost stamping as she spoke. "I'm sick of your cowardly spirit! *Can't!* I say you can, you shall, you must! I've borne with you, worked for you, given myself up to you— if you let your faint-heartedness deny this chance for bettering your life and Pen's, I'll never help you no more—I'll wash my hands of you. Pen must know every-thing, I say—everything. Either you or me shall tell her. You shan't deceive that girl, that has no guile in her. I'll hear no more of this fooling!"

Mrs. Hall was crying, not bitterly—that was not her way—not noisily, without sobs. She could only murmur in reply, without a touch of anger, that Jane was very hard.

"Hard! Ay, I never set up to be one of the soft ones; 'twas always you was that, Mary Chegwidden, always the one to coax and wheedle, while Jane got the rough side, and gave back hard for hard. But, all the same, I've cared for you and your good, and I'm caring now. Think of it, when you come to die and appear before the Lord, when you meet the father who thought the world of you, and was mercifully taken before he knew your shame—think of the difference it'll make if you can stand up before him and say, ' I died a wedded wife, father, with a right to a name.' I'm an ignorant woman, maybe, but I know what disgrace means, and I felt like to die when I found out that Mary Chegwidden had brought it on her father's honest memory."

" Hush, hush, then—oh, hush ! I'll try and bear it, if I must—if you'll not talk of deserting me, Jane ! Only don't say that I must let Pen know ! Why should she ? Of course I cannot leave her here—of course she must know what I go to London for. She must hear that I'm married ; but I can say that it was some one I knew long ago, before she was born ; she needn't hear it is her father."

"She must," Jane answered inflexibly. "If you won't tell her, I will. She must know everything."

There was no more resistance, no reply but the soft weeping. Mrs. Hall was too much used to being ruled in great things to fight with the iron will to which she had been wont to yield all her life long. If Jane said she must do anything she knew it was inevitable, whatever of terror or pain it might involve. At any rate she might delay a little—the call for action was not immediate ; at least she had some hours, a night, part of a day—before she must bring down the overwhelming, distracting torrent on her poor weak head. Jane grew gentle as the tears flowed, and no more words came. She brought tea, and made her drink it ; she soothed her with little silent services, keeping Penrose, by various devices, away from her mother.

At last the room was quite dark and silent, the other two in bed, and Mrs. Hall found herself alone with her memories, a crowding throng that clamoured all together for admission, picture after picture, more or less distinct, of the long procession of years since that early innocence of childhood and first youth, which was sweet and fragrant still to the woman of forty-three.

First rose that vision out of the past, the vision of the Cornish girl at home in the little house by the unresting sea. How fond she had been of every corner of the fishing village ; how wild and gay her childhood was, when she ran barefoot on the crisp shining sand, or over the weed-embroidered rocks, where the wet mussels shone blue when the sunshine rested on them, where the waves fretted themselves for ever in creamy foam against the hard-hearted cliffs, and the gulls screamed up above in the grey of the sky ! She had been a happy child then, at home, though "mother" was difficult to get on with at times, and apt to scold over wet clothes and spoilt shoes. Though Jane had always a will of her own, and was too old to be a playfellow, there were plenty of other girls and boys to race and shout with, to help look for lobsters and crabs, and to catch prawns in the pools. And when Captain Chegwidden came home it was a gala time. Molly had loved her handsome, good-natured sailor father with all her heart; he never gave her a rough word, she was "his pretty maid," his darling. He always stood between her and a scolding. She went to school, and was quick enough at her books. They were well-to-do folks, in their way, while Captain Chegwidden lived, and Molly did not know what hardship or trouble meant till she was fifteen years old, and her father and the boat went down one dreary October night. Then poverty knocked at the door. Jane went to service, and Mary had to stay at home and help her mother, to leave off both school and play, to fetch and carry, sew and clean, while all the while her pretty face grew prettier, and no one cared except a sailor boy here and there, who carried on a sort of rough courtship which the girl shrank from, half proudly and half shyly. She had been a little too well educated for them, and was not ready or bold enough with her tongue for the kind of flirtations they liked ; and her mother was strict, and kept frivolity at arm's length. Mrs. Chegwidden was a severe Methodist, and in her case, sorrow had produced a stricter rigour and more reserve of manner. She had never been a genial woman, and naturally was much less beloved than many a worse one. This was a sombre bit of life, the three years between fifteen and eighteen, which ended all childish days and joys for Mary Chegwidden, and brought none of the delights which succeed them in happier girlhoods.

Then another picture rose before the silence and darkness of the night, and the unsleeping eyes of the mind saw the first scene that heralded the crisis of her fate. A young Oxford man came one summer, five and twenty years ago, to lodge at Mrs. Chegwidden's cottage. He was a dark, handsome fellow, roving about the world to please himself, and had taken a whim in his head to revisit the country from which his ancestors had sprung. He was interested in antiquity, in old tradition, in the ancient legends and architecture of Cornwall. He was clever and bright and full of life; some one quite different from anybody Molly Chegwidden had ever known. He treated her with a light, easy courtesy, which made her somehow think of herself as she had never done before, and discover that she had a strong love of admiration, and a great desire to

please—at any rate, to please a gentleman
who was so good-looking and so kind,
whose eyes told her, if his lips didn't,
that she was the prettiest girl he had
seen for a long while; who was ridiculously lavish and generous with money,
satisfying Mrs. Chegwidden's wildest
wishes in that respect; who brought a
breeze of freshness in with him, who
had always something amusing or odd
to say, so that one felt really alive, not
as she often did, half so, with the best
of her mind asleep.

It was the brightest, sweetest, yet most
distracting month while he stayed, and
for the first time in her life the girl's
torpid heart awoke and thrilled into vivid
vitality. There never was anybody like
Mr. Trevenna; after knowing him there
was no looking at the sailors or the
traders of Trelewen. She was a soft-
spoken, soft-eyed, pretty young thing then
—the middle-aged woman remembered

still how she had looked in a hat with
red ribbons in it, with her crisp dark hair
curling about her brown smiling face, and
how Mr. Trevenna had gazed at her, with
his bright observant eyes soft with a new
expression—she remembered even a little
whisper, " Bravo, Molly, the hat and the
face together are quite too irresistible."
It was Sunday night, and the boys and
girls went on the headland together after
their wont on summer Sundays—every
Jill had her Jack except Mary Chegwidden, and she walked alone till Mr.
Trevenna overtook her, and persuaded
her to scramble down to the rocks to
watch the tide come in. Oh, happy day,
happy day that never came again, and
had no perfect fellow in all the years
that followed, or all that went before !

There was no looking forwards or back-
wards, but a pause, a bliss, that weighed
and considered nothing, and seemed to
mean no more than just the short span

of inconsequent delight. Mary had no plans, no expectations, no fears, hardly any hopes. She only knew that she was eighteen years old, that she looked prettier than she ever had done before, and that the most perfect companion in the world sat beside her, and made the time pass like a sunbeam. To be sure, like all happy hours, this had to be paid for. Directly after, it seemed to her, came the miserable day of parting, and the blankness of going back to her work-a-day world again with all the zest of living out of it, nothing but sulkily done labour slurred through, constant scolding, and a dreary sense that there was nothing to be looked forward to till next summer, when Mr. Trevenna would come again. And that summer had come, and Mr. Trevenna too ; a little less delightful perhaps at first, rather more guarded and distant, not so apt to meet her wistful eyes, more careful to prevent any suspicion of a flirtation. But Fate had been too strong for him and her—they like to call it fate who stumble over their path of life. Her mother had been suddenly taken ill, and, after only a day's suffering, had died.

Mary Chegwidden was quite alone in the world, for her only sister was out of reach, having gone abroad with her mistress. Alone, frightened, dependent, clinging to him as if he were the only friend left her, Richard Trevenna was not too particular in the modes of his consolation; he had strong passions, and took the usual cynical masculine view of pretty, inferior, yielding girls. When Mrs. Chegwidden was buried he paid all her debts, left the cottage and furniture to be sold, and took the daughter of the dead woman away with him to see something of a new, intoxicating world. Mary never, then or now, was able to feel the righteous wrath of a woman deceived and seduced. Indignation and self-assertion were alike impossible to her plastic, timid, unimaginative soul. She simply gave way directly to love and to him ; she hardly expected him to marry her, though, as she was really at heart a good girl and a modest one, with absolutely nothing of the meretricious in her simple nature, she was ashamed of having done what her dead father and mother would have thought a bitter disgrace.

If either had been alive, she probably would never have yielded ; but there was no one to care, and be shamed, except that elder sister, whom she had almost forgotten. It did not seem to matter much to any one, and she loved Mr. Trevenna in a humble, unexacting, adoring fashion. He could not do anything wicked in her eyes. She was just the woman whose proper destiny had been to be a quiet, comfortable, indolent matron, content with husband and children whatever they might be, slipping gently through

life without being of much importance
anywhere.   She had never got her proper
footing since she missed this fate.   It had
been very delightful at first ; they travelled
about for a year, and then settled down
in Paris for a time, just for a whim of
Trevenna's.   Here Penrose was born ;
here change again — the thing of all
others she naturally feared—came upon
her, and here she ended the dream of an
impossible happiness.

No one but Richard Trevenna knew
what made it hateful to him to go on as
he had been doing.   It had not taken
many months, it is true, to put an end to
his first raptures and his transitory passion
for Mary Chegwidden.   There was not
enough in her to change passion into love.
He was kind to her, fond of her, considerate about her long after he left off
being her lover at heart.   But there was
an external influence beyond this alteration in feeling which made him break with

the connection, something which not only severed this, but also completely destroyed the illusion and charm of existence, which made him the pronounced cynic, misanthrope, and bitter man of the world which he became from that time. He had never been a man of high principle, or one who followed high ideals; but something malign and cruel entered into his life then that had never been there before. He had wronged one woman, and another avenged her. Who it was, what it was, Mary never knew; she only felt and suffered by the results. She suffered, but not as acutely as another kind of disposition would; her nature seemed too soft to be broken; she did not feel an overpowering surprise, or an unendurable despair; she had her bonnie little girl, in whose companionship there was no sting. She had grown frightened and oppressed by Trevenna's moods, his uncaressing coldness, his sarcasms, his aloofness. She knew, without bitterness towards him for the knowledge, that she was not the woman to satisfy or keep his heart; it was a grief, but not a cruel one, to come to an end of the brief dream that this love might last. She still cared for him, for though her feelings were not intense, they were constant, but his presence no longer gave her happiness; on the contrary, she was uneasy and miserable with him under the perpetual sense of inadequacy and dissatisfaction. Her maternal instinct was the strongest passion left in her; the rest seemed all exhausted or frightened away. She acquiesced with floods of tears, but without a word of remonstrance or blame to his sudden decree of separation. He was what the world calls generous in his provision for her; she should never know the poverty again in which he found her. He probably satisfied his conscience with this at the time. He parted with her easily enough. His child he had never much noticed; he did not care for children. She was healthy and quiet, and her mother doted on her, that was all he knew.

After this parting, when for a time Mary Chegwidden, who had taken the name of Mrs. Hall, was staying in London, circumstances strangely threw her into communication with her sister Jane. From that time they had never been parted. Jane was angry and grieved to find what had happened, but not surprised. The people at Trelewen had told her of Mary's disappearance with "the gentleman;" the rough Cornish woman had never hoped to learn that her sister was "an honest wife." She felt the disgrace, and reproached Mary at first with outspoken harshness; but there was no keeping up wrath with a gentle fluid creature who had never a word to answer it with, who only cried and was silent.

Jane had no one else to love; she liked to command and arrange, she had a strongly clannish feeling for her own. She took up her abode with her sister when she moved into the cottage at Copsley which Mr. Hamley had to let, but as her servant, she insisted on that, folks should not talk if she could help it. Mary must pass as a respectable widow lady with a maid. She had rubbed off a good deal of her rustic plainness, and had always been better educated and more refined than her elder sister, who had not had her early chances, and was altogether cast in a harder, rougher mould. In private Jane might rule and scold when she liked; before people she was the familiar old servant only.

This had been Mary Chegwidden's life. It was not exactly a tragedy, though a woman of intense feeling might have made one of it. It was, but for one great event, a quiet monotony, and she had grown accustomed to it, and, in her way, happy. Yet there was one element of

tragedy, one great terror that passed
beyond the borders of the commonplace.
This was the dread with which the mere
idea of Penrose knowing all her past had
inspired her. Penrose was her conscience,
her soul. Left to herself, she would have
calmly accepted her position, and been
little troubled by remorse or shame. Her
conscience had never been a restless or
uneasy one, but her instinctive under-
standing of Penrose's widely different
nature put a new aspect on everything,
and made her vaguely realize how her
daughter would have looked upon her
past. The strong, courageous, uncompromising spirit which had come like a
child of another world into her life, the
absolute truthfulness and purity of the
nature she could only understand by affection, was a new revelation. If Penrose
turned against her she should just lie
down and die. Yet Jane said Penrose
must know, that she must go through this

double ordeal, must meet Richard Trevenna once more after all this waste of
years, must let Penrose into the secret
which she had hoped to carry away with
her into the silence of the grave. And
if Jane was inexorable, as she knew too
well she would be, there was no help for
it. She lay all night awake, staring blankly
out into the dark, keeping her vigil with
memory and fear, poor soul, till her exhausted body could bear the watch no
longer, and sleep came—sleep like a
child's, undreaming and unbroken.

Jane came in to call her in the morning
as usual, but let her sleep on.

"Poor girl!" she said, forgetting that
the soft curly hair on the pillow was mixed
with grey, and with a sudden tenderness of
pity; "let her sleep her fill. It'll be none
so bright a waking, and Molly was never
the one to stand against trouble. But it's
for the best. It's got to be—and soon.
That man must have his answer to-day."

CHAPTER X.

MRS. HALL did not come downstairs that morning, but Penrose was not anxious. She had slept badly, Jane said, with one of her headaches and a little palpitation, and was taking what rest she could. She pretty often stayed in bed in the early part of the day. Her constitution was languid, and though her health was not bad, her strength was never great, and she easily sank into a kind of lymphatic indolence. Penrose had enough to do to keep her busy. It was raining, and she could not go to sketch on the common as she intended; so, when her household tasks were over, she set up the easel in the light, unfurnished little room which she used for her own purposes. But she had not begun to paint when Jane came in rather slowly, with something in her face that struck the girl with a kind of vague fear, something grave, uncertain, embarrassed.

"What is it, Jane?" she asked her quickly, letting her brush fall as she turned to face her. "Mother's not ill?"

"No, she's not ill—only a bit disturbed and unhappy. I've something to say to you, Penrose, that your mother's fain to leave to my telling. I've tried my best to persuade her to say it for herself; but you know just how she is—so easily frightened, and so chary to speak. Come, sit by me here, and I'll try and tell you, as well as I can, what you've got to know. You'll not be hard on your mother, Pen, whatever's been and over, will you now?"

The unusual pleading and indecision in

the voice that was apt to be so short and abruptly resolute startled Penrose. She fixed an intently earnest gaze on the dark eyes that sank under hers as they had never done before.

"Why should I? How could I be hard on mother?" the clear voice said, with a thrill in it. "You know well enough that I never could, Jane. She's not afraid of that, surely, surely not!"

"She *is* afraid—mortal afraid, poor soul! But I tell her she needn't be. You'll not turn against her whatever—I know you'll not. But it's a difficult task to begin—a sore thing to tell of a woman to her own daughter. I'd fain have let it alone, but since she will have it so, she must. You know who your mother's father was?"

"Yes. Captain Chegwidden."

"Ay. Her name was — is — Mary Chegwidden; but what you don't know is, that he was *my* father too."

"Your father! You are my mother's *sister!*"

"I am your mother's only sister. We were born of the same father but of another mother. I'm more than ten years older. We were both born to Trelewen, and bred by the sea that wrecked him and began our troubles. I've passed as your servant; but I'm your flesh and blood, and the Lord knows I've loved you, and shall love you till I die. You two are all the kin I have. But I'm only telling you this to make you feel as I've a right to speak of things that go deep in both your lives; so as you needn't feel shamed by my knowing all I do, more than you've known. The time's come now when you can't go on any longer in ignorance. It'll hurt you, child, and I hate to hurt you; but there's no other way. You know nothing of your father —not a word; she's kept silence to you. You think him dead."

" And he is not dead ? "

" No ; he's not dead. Your mother has been called a widow—called Mrs. Hall ; but she's neither one nor the other. Your father's name is Trevenna, Richard Trevenna, and he's alive this day."

" Trevenna ! Is that my name ? "

Jane breathed hard. A curious look of compunction and pity came over her stern features. She paused a moment before she said, in a suppressed and altered voice, " No, my dear ; you've no right to his name, no more than to any other. Your mother was no wedded wife."

Penrose did not start nor cry. She was white to the lips—a strange whiteness which crept over the healthy brown of her clear skin. She sat perfectly still, and stared straight beyond all visible objects, as if she saw a vision of pain.

" No wedded wife ! " She repeated the words slowly to herself. " No wedded wife ! Then what am I ? What do they

call the children of women who are not
wedded wives ? "

Ah, they bear an ugly name ! Penrose
was a proud girl, and the thought ran like
a fire through her. She was content to be
obscure ; she would not mind if she had to
work for her living—no, not even in the
humblest fashion ; but she was *not* content
to be shamed ! She shivered, and a
crimson flush dyed all her face and neck.
For the moment it was of herself, not of
her mother, that she thought and suffered.
Her pride was outraged and stung into
what seemed to be almost rage. Jane's
next slow, difficultly uttered words roused
her into a change of feeling.

" It's dreadful to your mother for you to
know. Poor soul ! she loves you so dear.
She's afraid you'll turn against her, now
you know. But you'll not—you'll not ; I
know you'll not ! "

The rigid whiteness which had succeeded
the crimson in the young face, and made

it almost terrible to see, passed like a cloud. Penrose rose suddenly to her feet.

"Oh, poor mother! Poor mother!" she said, in a stifled tone, broken with an anguish of pity; "for *her* to be afraid of *me!*" She went towards the door quickly, but Jane caught her arm.

"Stay a moment—bless you for being in haste to comfort her—but I've more to tell. If something hadn't happened, you'd never have known; she'd never have let you, for she had a terrible fear of it. I've promised to tell you all about it, and you must hear. This Mr. Trevenna, your father, who ought to have been her husband three and twenty years agone, he's a rich man—what folks call a gentleman; and he's written to her after all this time. He's willing now to give her his name. When he dies, you and she will be rich women. Ah, don't start away now as if you didn't mean to hear! I'm not saying as you would care a bit for that—as if his money could pay for all that's past and gone; but the thing must be, and you will help her go through with it. It's her right —though I know it's late enough to talk of rights, and nothing he can do can set straight what was crooked to begin with. It was this letter that came last night and upset her so—the time had come when she couldn't keep her secret from you any longer. It's been like shedding the very blood of her heart to let go of it. You'll be good to your mother—you'll comfort her. Say you will now, darling!" She caught hold of the girl, and kissed her suddenly and fervently, putting into that one kiss the silent love of many a year.

Penrose put her arms round the thin shoulders, bent with willing toil, and laid her cold face against the hard, lined cheek. No one had caressed Jane Chegwidden for the best part of a lifetime. There was no need of words. A strong new sense of kindred, of fellowship, stirred in

each heart—there was something of re-
semblance in the two, something of the
noble fortitude and faithful strength of an
ancient race. Each knew well how to
trust the other—to the death, if need be.
Jane's heart beat with a sorrowful joy.
She had been alone all her life, had spent
herself without hope of reward, and suddenly God had given her the sweet gift of
a new love. It was born in a moment of
trouble, for she was moved with a pity
that was almost torture ; but she knew
that it would turn into a glad possession
to brighten the loneliness of the years to
come.

"God bless thee, my dear !" she said,
passing her ·hard hand softly over the
thick hair. "However it happens I don't
know ; but you're one of the chosen—good
right through to the heart of you. Your
mother needn't be afraid."

When Penrose opened the door and
came swiftly to her mother, Mrs. Hall

started up in bed with a cry that was almost a wail. It sounded like a cry for pity. Whether that or not, it was silenced on her girl's heart. Penrose clasped the poor trembling woman closely, warmly, passionately.

" Mothie, dear mothie!" she whispered, in her tenderest voice, using the old baby, endearing name. " I know — I know! You were never afraid that I should be hard on you! It's better I should know, dear. You'll be glad there's nothing between you and me, after a while. You've always got me, mothie, whatever may happen, and you mustn't doubt that I'll stand by you. You'll never, never, never doubt that ? "

Her words, and the knowledge that this revelation—the one she had most dreaded and shrank from—was over, and that her daughter knew and yet did not turn away from her, were like a cordial to the timid heart. She revived in a moment. Something in the very weakness and inadequacy of her nature enabled her to be her calm, everyday self again as soon as she had cried away all her tears ; up and about her little insignificant works before Penrose had realized what had happened, and had faced the new conditions of her life. The strangely different, the infinitely deeper and stronger nature, could not adapt itself so easily to such a change of thought.

Penrose needed all her courage to bear the loss of so many ideals of her life. Her father was not dead ; that imaginary father whose picture she had made out of nothing, about whom the very completeness of silence and ignorance she had been in had left more scope to imagination, had never existed, had gone out of her life, and instead, there was an idea that was terrible and abhorrent to her. She had no blame, no severity for her mother—it was no novelty to have to make allowances,

and to know how weak a thing it was she
was used to love and care for, but the
thought of this new father was hateful to
her.   She would fain have thrust it from
her ; but it would come back.   She could
not bear to think that all these years there
had been some one living who had spoilt
and defaced her mother's life, some one
who was nothing, yet everything to them.
And now he had come forward with this
strange idea of righting all the wrong that
never could be righted, and she could not
keep her mother out of his reach.   They
must submit to his power, be beholden to
him for horrible benefactions—it might
even become a wrong to hate the very
thought of him.   Penrose had the stern
vein in her which had descended from
some of those peasant ancestors, the same
that was in Jane Chegwidden, and absolutely wanting in her own mother; she was
only never stern to any one she loved or
pitied.   She hated cruelty, she abhorred

the coarse, sensual, and malign vices, she
had the spirit in her of a young knight-
errant, the capacity for martyrdom. And
now she had to submit her proud, angry,
pure soul to the brand of disgrace. The
knowledge of her mother's past was to her
like some sin of her own doing—the shame
of that easy yielding, of the long acquies-
cence and contentment under the sense
of it, ached at her heart with an almost
unendurable pain. She bore it as the one
who had done the sin could never have
done. She felt it as her mother had not,
even when it was fresh ; it was a bitter
consciousness that stained every memory
that had been calm and dear. She had to
bear the loss, the sting, the pain, in perfect
silence ; no one should ever have to say
of her that she had felt so of her mother.
Perhaps Jane guessed at it a little in her
rough crude way, by that sort of instinct
which likeness of nature gives ; but nothing
of confidence passed between them after

the first.   She would not let Penrose treat
her in any way differently.   She was determined to be the servant, not the kinswoman.
" No one shall have any call to talk about
a change," she said ; " you shan't alter one
mite to me."   No one saw anything strange,
therefore.   The internal earthquake that
had shaken them all was unknown outside
the walls of the cottage.

   Mrs. Hall wrote her letter to Mr.
Hamley, putting herself and all arrangements for her future absolutely in his
hands.   He was to take lodgings, to
tell her when to come to town, to make
everything as easy as was possible for her.
This was her way ; when there was any
one ready and willing to take responsibility, to guide and to serve her, she
threw herself and her whole future im-
plicitly upon him.   Since this thing had
to be, and she must face the ordeal, some
one must help her through, some one
must be the director of it ; she could bear

anything with passive patience if she were
not expected to do more than bear.
Her greatest dread was meeting Richard
Trevenna face to face after all this quiet
stretch of years, during which she had had
the time not to forget, but to grow accustomed to a brooding memory that was no
longer painful. Whenever she thought of
this she trembled with a nameless fear and
shrinking, yet the soft tenacity of her
feelings at times mingled strangely with
the terror a curious, faint longing for the
very thing she trembled at. The ashes
of the past were absolutely dead ; but there
was just this difference between the man
and the woman—in one case they were
cold as clay, in the other the ashes still
held the last lingering warmth of a fire
that time had slowly burnt away.

Trevenna had taken up this long forgotten tie simply because his conscience
had been stirred by friendship, by a half-
revived faith, by the approach of death, to

a sense of a duty which his mind could not reject. He had not the very smallest remnant of sentiment remaining for the past that was only a burden to him. He prepared to go through with it with a stoical coldness, and half-affected cynicism which was easier to keep up than any other attitude. It was perhaps an act of mere insanity, he was giving way to his old friend's quixotism and overstrained ideas of right; but, since he had given his word to do it, he must go through with all the inevitable disagreeables as grimly and indifferently as his philosophy would allow. There was one of those lulls in his disease which often make a deceitful calm for a time; he was tolerably free for the moment from physical pain, and able to take exertions which would have usually prostrated him. He took no one into his confidence but Mr. Grey—no other soul besides knew when he left home where he was going, and no one imagined that he had any particular object in the suddenly arranged visit to London. He took rooms for himself and for Grey in a quiet hotel, his manservant was left at Redwood; and on the very evening he reached town he had arranged for a meeting with the woman who was to be his wife at Mr. Hamley's chambers.

It was the briefest, strangest, coldest meeting between two who had not seen each other for more than twenty years, who had parted when they were in their prime, the one a handsome man something over thirty, the other a mere girl in the bloom and beauty of life; now he was a bent, sallow, grey-headed, hollow-eyed invalid, who looked more like seventy than fifty odd years; she was a stout, pale, hesitating, commonplace middle-aged woman, with frightened furtive eyes and hesitating voice. They touched each other's hands, and a few strange cold words were interchanged. Each seemed to the other a different creature from the self of those old days. He told her his intentions for the immediate and the later future, she humbly and almost speechlessly acquiesced.

"I will execute a will as soon as the affair is over," he said, in his harsh, weary voice, "leaving my property to you for life—to your daughter afterwards. There shall be a proper acknowledgment of our relations to each other. You will not wish to alter your home or way of life at present, I imagine. When my death is expected, it will be better for you to come to Redwood and to take your place at once there. I will see that you are properly considered."

He stopped, and was silent, as if searching for what more to say; she suddenly raised her swollen lids, and gazed at him with a curious wistfulness. Was this all, after what was past and gone between them? These frosty, business-like sentences, these stern unfriendly glances ? She did not know what she expected, what she wanted, only something lay cold at her heart, and she blindly and vaguely groped about for words to express the formless desire for a gentler conclusion.

"You said you were ill," she faltered out, in bald hesitating phrases, which she felt incapable of bettering. "Are you sure I can't do anything for you ? I—we —don't you want some one to look after you, if—since you are not well ? "

"Thank you," he said, with a cold courtesy that froze the stumbling words ; "but I am well enough looked after. I am not an agreeable invalid, and I should be sorry to demand anything from you. It could not be a happy situation for either of us. I am willing to acknowledge that I wronged you, and therefore I will do what I can—though late. I will give you my name, as I said. The position of my widow will be better for you than that of

my wife could be. No one need know
anything more than that we were separated
long ago. Mr. Hamley has settled everything so as to avoid all unnecessary disturbance or unpleasantness. I do not
think that we need say any more. I am
not a man of feeling; we shall find this
least disagreeable if we treat it 'as mere
business."

She could not answer him; a dumb pain,
half fear of him, half the reviving remembrance of what had been once and never
could be any more, a foolish feminine ache
as she realized how utterly her day had
gone by—the little bright day that had
been overclouded so early,—all these shape-
less feelings stirred her slow heart, but
brought no words to the unready tongue.
Once she had clung to this cold, stern, grey
stranger, who was and was not the Richard
Trevenna of the old Trelewen days. Once
he had kissed her, had called her soft
foolish names—his bird, his pet, his pretty

Molly ; now there was a great gulf fixed between them, across which not one tender message could ever pass. Long ago it would have been a pride, a bliss to bear his name ; then, when there was love between them, he denied her the bliss. Now, when love was dead, and she dare not even shed tears on its grave, he threw her the gift that had lost all value. He had been cruel in the past, when she forgave him without a struggle ; now, when he meant to right the old wrongs, she felt him cruelest of all. He had better have left her in the dull contented quiet of her later years !

"I think," he went on, in that cool indifferent voice, hard as wrought iron, "if it suits you, it would be best for you to leave Copsley. Things might leak out there, you could travel, perhaps, a little, or make a temporary home somewhere till you have to consider how best to manage. Wherever you are I shall always hear through Hamley."

"Yes. I shall leave Copsley," she said wearily, looking on the ground. "I dare say it will be best."

"I shall increase your income."

"I don't want it. I have more than I want now," she interposed, more quickly than she had spoken before. "I never spend all."

"I had rather," he returned imperiously. "You can put it by for—for your daughter."

"For *my* daughter!" The words escaped almost involuntarily with the first tone of reproach. The accent did not escape him.

"Well, for *our* daughter; but, since I don't know her, you must forgive my feeling her to be yours only."

"Will you—will you see her?"

"No, no," he said quickly, with harsh emphasis; "what use in that? She would only detest me—naturally. She knows, of course?"

" Yes ; I—I had to tell her."

" I will do what justice I can for her.
I will arrange, if you please, for her also
to take the name of Trevenna in future.
I need not detain you any longer now ;
you perfectly understand all our arrangements ? "

" Yes."

" Then we need not discuss it any
further. If anything strikes you, if you
desire any alteration made, any addition
to what I have stated, or if I have made
any part of what I have to ask you to go
through needlessly unpleasant, you will
let me know. I am anxious to save you
what I can."

" No ; there's nothing — nothing you
could do," she returned, in the same dull,
dragging voice, slowly rising to her feet
and preparing to go. She felt there was
nothing possible, since things were as they
were, since he was he ; there was no more
to be said, no more to be done. He was,

perhaps, not to blame for this weight of lead on her heart. Twenty years' alienation! And before that his love had gone from her. She wondered how it must feel to be a woman no longer young and fair, who yet was beloved, who was the wife of a man's heart. She stole one furtive glance up at him; he looked so haggard, so old, weary, and world-worn, she was almost as sorry for him as for herself, and she blamed neither the one nor the other. Dead, dead and cold, the old love of their youth; but still the soft-hearted woman yearned with a pity for it and for him that almost simulated the dead love that could not return. She put out her hesitating, tremulous hand. It had just felt his when they met; but now, when he would have withdrawn his again after the briefest touch possible, she let her fingers fasten on his for a moment's space. She had no weapon against his invincible coldness, but if he had lost it for an instant, she could have fallen at his feet and wept.

"Good-bye, Mary," he said, and even the bare sound of her name, which she used to think his voice made as sweet as a caress, caused a thrill in her veins; she was grateful for even that coldly spoken word. She only answered it by one plaintive look, which might have been pathetic if she had not been a stout, heavy, middle-aged woman, in whom sentiment seemed ludicrous, and they parted without another word. The ordeal was over! She was relieved—as glad as she could be of anything—but the slow tears would keep rising as fast as she wiped them off, as she drove back alone to her lodgings; and she could have told no one—she hardly knew herself—what made them come. She only knew she had missed something that life once seemed to have promised her, that she had nothing to hope for beyond the mere blankness of a peace that was half insensibility. This was what she must meet the future with ; the only actual sweetness left besides was in the assurance that Penrose would never leave off loving her.

CHAPTER XI.

MRS. FOLLIOTT was busy in a most exemplary fashion one morning over yards of uninviting brown calico, when Miss Babb burst in upon her in the eager possession of a piece of news.

"Good morning, Mrs. Folliott! Excuse my being so early. I was out for my constitutional, and thought I must first look in to ask if you've heard that the Halls are leaving Copsley all of a sudden."

"My dear Miss Babb! Leaving Copsley? Why, their term can't be up till midsummer, and no one has heard a word of it."

" No, that's the extraordinary part; but I always *did* say there was something odd about Mrs. Hall. You'll bear me out that I did. For all her demure, creep-mouse ways, I'm convinced she's got something in her past that no one has any idea of. She went to London last week; they all three went, and only took a bag or two, for I saw them go to the station, and expected they'd be back before now. Well, when I went past the cottage, who should I meet coming out but Jane—locking the door after her, going to the village for something. Of course I stopped her to ask how her mistress and Penrose were, and if they were back. No, she said; nor coming neither. They'd made up their minds to go about a bit; she's come to see what luggage they wanted, and was going to Beale's, the house-agent, about leaving the cottage and furniture. She was, as she always is, as silent and glum as possible, not a thing to be got out of her. But I have a shrewd suspicion that Mrs. Hall has got married again."

" Married again ! What makes you think that ? It isn't at all likely, at her age, and not even well-preserved ; and there has never been any one at the cottage."

" No ; but for all that—now just listen— Jane had a paper and some letters in her hand, and was going evidently to post them. After she had gone on, I saw that she had dropped one, so I picked it up to pop in the box for her. Now, how do you think it was directed ? The ' Mrs. Hall, Heathside Cottage, Copsley,' was crossed out—by Jane, I suppose—and redirected to ' Mrs. Trevenna, Bedford Place, London.' How comes it that Mrs. Hall's letter should be sent on to Mrs. Trevenna, unless she is married again, or she never was Mrs. Hall, but passed under a wrong name ? Didn't I always say it was mysterious her having no relations in the world, and never any one to see her?"

"Trevenna? Trevenna? Now, how do I know the name?" mused Mrs. Folliott, knitting her brow with an effort of memory, and ignoring Miss Babb's conscious triumph in her own sagacity. "It seems familiar. Oh, I remember now, there was a friend of Mr. Folliott's of that name—Trevenna—Trevenna—it was some one he knew, I am sure, long ago, that I've heard him speak of. Somebody in the Midlands, I believe, or he met him at college. I must ask."

"But isn't it strange now? What can you make out of it?"

"It *is* odd. But I can hardly think Mrs. Hall can have married again."

"Well, if not, depend on it she never was Mrs. Hall, and has taken another name. Jane knows all about it, of that I'm convinced. Jane has always seemed deep in her confidence."

"Well, at any rate, there's nothing mysterious or underhand about *Penrose.* She always has been particularly open and honest—as far as one can judge, that is."

"Oh yes, there's nothing wrong about her," Miss Babb agreed, with something of kindliness mingling with her inquisitive eagerness. "I like the girl; she's been very nice to me, and I've never seen anything deceitful about her, I will say *that.* But as to the mother——" A comprehensive shake of the head conveyed more than a host of words.

"Well, well, there *may* be some explanation of it, if we only knew," Mrs. Folliott said, rallying the orthodox expression of benign indulgence, which she considered became one "in her position."

"Ah, charity's all very well," Miss Babb retorted nippingly, "but there's a point where it becomes idiotic. I'm convinced, explanation or no explanation, that there's something *very queer* about the whole business, and about Mrs. Hall, or whatever she calls herself. Who knows what sort of a character we've all been associating with ? "

Mrs. Folliott had some sense of humour, the expression of pious horror on the elderly lady's hard-lined face forced a smile to her lips.

"Well, dear Miss Babb, no one can be said to have *associated* very much with Mrs. Hall, since she never would be on easy terms with any one. *You* were the most at the cottage, and no one can suppose it's done you any harm!"

"I don't know that—one can't be too particular. Whenever there's a mystery one generally finds it to be a discreditable one, that's my experience, and a mystery there certainly is about this woman. What made her so shy and reserved, I'd like to know, if it wasn't a consciousness of being unfit for virtuous female society? Well, I'm sorry for Penrose. Of course it's possible I may even have been deceived in her; but I hardly think it. No one could seem to be so open and truthful, and be a hypocrite. No, I do believe, whatever the mother may be, Penrose is a good girl. You mark my words, Mrs. Folliott, no one will see Mrs. Hall's face in Copsley again. Jane's been round paying all her bills—they didn't amount to much, for she didn't run up accounts, I'll say *that* for her."

"Oh, and you may say more," Mrs. Folliott interposed, still with her charitable expression on; "while she lived here —and she was quite a young woman when she came, not more than five-and-twenty, I suppose—there has been nothing in her life to cause the very smallest scandal. Nobody could have led a quieter or more retired one."

" No, that's what I say was so mysterious and unnatural; that is what makes me sure there is a secret. And she never wore widow's weeds, not even mourning. I thought that odd at the time. Well, I'll wish you good morning. If I find out anything more I'll let you know."

At luncheon Mrs. Folliott casually asked her husband if he had not once known some one called Trevenna.

"Yes, to be sure, my dear. I was at Christ Church with Dick Trevenna, if you mean him—a wild, clever, queer sort of young fellow. I lost sight of him afterwards for several years, when I met him in Oxford by chance. He was living then at a place of his some miles out—I forget the name of it—property he'd inherited. He was a good deal altered, old-looking, quite grey and worn, though he was some years younger than I, and I thought myself still in the prime of life then—under forty. We did not get on particularly well; he had a sarcastic, caustic way with him, which was a new development, and not a pleasant one."

" Was he a married man ? "

" I'm sure I don't know, my dear; I

did not ask. As I say, he did not impress me agreeably. I hadn't much talk with him. What makes you ask about Tre-venna now ?"

Mrs. Folliott discreetly forbore to enter into any particulars "before the girls," about whom she had a theory of her own not borne out by facts. She chose to think them innocent young things, guarded from all the darker facts of life, while in reality the Miss Folliotts were specimens of our nineteenth-century young ladies, knowing most things, shocked at nothing, and quite capable of holding their own with anybody of either sex. Such harmless delusions are common with parents. When she had her husband alone she gave him Miss Babb's bit of gossip, with her own comment that "it was certainly very odd."

Mr. Folliott laughed with manly scepticism. "Is that all that you and old Babb have got to make a story out of ? Probably there's nothing in it at all. Mrs. Hall was never in the habit of taking the town into her confidence, and Jane is a very silent woman, objecting to be *drawn.* And as for the name—there are more Trevennas in the world than one."

"Oh yes; that's nothing. It was only that I was sure I had some association with the name. But, say what you like, I can't help keeping my own opinion that Mrs. Hall, or whatever she is called, has behaved in a very strange way."

Mrs. Folliott was a contradictory woman, liking to hold her own. She had taken the side of "charity" with Miss Babb; now, when her husband seemed incredulous, she was all for the idea of a mystery.

"We shall never see *Mrs. Hall* again here, take my word for it," she said, nodding her head; "and no one will miss her."

"Oh, I don't know that; she was good to some of the poor people, and her

daughter more so. Penrose behaved
wonderfully kindly to that poor thing that
died. She is rather a strong-willed young
woman, but I like Penrose."

"Well, so do I, well enough. But
Penrose and her mother are two very
different people. I never saw mother and
daughter less alike."

"Are you going to make a mystery out
of that, Charlotte?"

"It's all very well to laugh, Mr. Folliott,
but I am generally right in my sur-
mises."

"Oh yes, women are always right.
Have your own way, my dear, cling
to your mystery, I've no objection at
all. Only there's one subscription less
on all my charities if Mrs. Hall does not
turn up again."

Mrs. Folliott was triumphantly confirmed in her opinion of her infallibility
when the spring and summer passed and
neither Mrs. Hall, Penrose, nor Jane

reappeared in Copsley. The cottage was
let at midsummer, the furniture was sold,
and their place knew them no more.
Penrose's slender, tall, vigorous figure was
no longer seen walking swiftly over the
common or about the village. Her few
friends missed her. The old artist who
had given her lessons in painting, and
whose comrade she had been, in a frank,
cordial, almost boyish fashion, was the
one who most lamented the want of her
sympathetic companionship. He had been
fond of her, in his gruff, undemonstrative
way, since she was a little tomboy of a girl,
doing daring feats in climbing and leaping,
with a thick pigtail down her back, and
he felt the lonely autumn of his days more
cheerless and chill for the absence of the
girl who was so eager to learn and get on
in the study of landscape painting and
near knowledge of nature. He felt forgotten, too, and was inclined to be more
cynical than before in his views of friend-

ship and women, till he got a short, rather
sad, but cordial note of thanks and farewell.
She should not be living in Copsley again,
she said. They were travelling about a
little, and should most likely settle down
somewhere else, but she should never
forget those happy sketching days, the
pleasantest in all her life. She hoped he
would not forget his "affectionate and
grateful pupil, Penrose." There was no
second name. She sent him with the
letter a new colour-box, but she gave him
no address, so that he could neither
acknowledge it nor thank her ; but he was
glad in his way to know that she was not
fickle and ungrateful, like the rest of her
sex.

The old women in the village, whom
Penrose had visited and enriched with her
little gifts and friendly cordiality, were
loud in their wails. " Her was a nice
young lady, her was ; not like them gals
from the Vicarage as never have no time

to set down and chat, but jest pop in, give
un a track or a mite o' tea, and off again
with a 'Good mornin',' as if they was
queen. No, Miss Pen 'ud come and stop,
maybe half an hour, and listen so kind
to all one had to say, with summat nice
and cheering at the end, so hearty-like
and nateral. Her could ill be spared in a
place like this'n, where the ladies be so
high and stand-off!"

These were the friends Penrose left
behind, these; and all the wistful curs
whom nobody noticed, save to kick out
of the way, the forlorn cats who snatched
a precarious living with teeth and claws,
and who were too downhearted to keep
their fur smooth, the dirty children, who,
like the mongrels and despised pussies,
got more kicks than halfpence, these
missed her loudly or mutely. She had
been the friend and champion of the poor,
the weak, the ugly and unloved, the
black sheep of the community; these

dreary lives were the drearier for the absence of her kind clear glance and her strong helpful hand. She made no gap in the gay set or the "society people;" she had never been of them.

CHAPTER XII.

PENROSE, her mother, and Jane Chegwidden drifted from London in an aimless sort of way. Mrs. Trevenna, as Jane perpetually called her, to accustom her to the strange sound of the name which at first made her tremble and flush, had been slow to express any decided wish as to her whereabouts, except that of not returning "home," as she still called Copsley. She shrank from inquiries, from starting there under a new title which she could hardly yet bear calmly. She thought at first she would stay on in London, but very soon the noise, the heartless bustle, the intense loneliness of the alien crowd became hateful to the country-bred woman of narrow, limited tastes and sympathies. Penrose did not dislike town life, though she was heavy-hearted at times; something of the fascination of its size, its fullness, the new studies open to her of art and of mankind, seized hold of her imagination. She liked to walk alone in the crowds, and to look round at the infinite variety which was spread everywhere in a vast panorama before her thoughtful, serious eyes. She was utterly unconscious of any disagreeableness as of any wrong in going about like this, she was absolutely secure behind the shield of her valiant maidenhood. It was not, as we know, the innocence of ignorance; there were sights and sounds which she understood with shuddering keenness, but she had no fear herself of insult or defilement. She took her way alone, an unprotected girl, not twenty-three, down the Strand in the evening, and if any man looked at her with evil eyes even these did not read her wrong. She was young, there was beauty of its own kind in her great grey eyes, her clear skin, straight profile, and abundant hair, as in her tall, well-formed figure, erect in the unconscious grace of health and strength, but it was not the beauty which allures the street lounger; there was something of sternness about her, she had no arts, no side glances, no pretty girlish wiles. Once she involuntarily laid her hand on a half-drunken, hysterical girl, who was beginning the shrieking, foul-mouthed invective, which is the precursor of a street scene, and looking full in the degraded, flushed young face that had been pretty, just said a word or two full of soothing compassion. The girl's bloodshot, angry eyes fell upon those large, kind, crystal-clear ones that looked at her without loathing or hate, and a sudden rush of softening tears came.

They were half maudlin, no doubt, but they sprang from some fount of sweetness not yet quite dried up in the impure soul.

" You will go home quietly, won't you ? " the voice said, the strong, low-toned, compassionate voice. " And if I can help you in any way I shall be glad."

" Bless you, miss," the girl said sobbing, as Penrose drew her into a quiet entry. " You can't do me no good; but I'll go quietly because you've spoken kind to me, and no one never does that now— no one like you—— "

Virtue had gone out of the pure woman, and the other went away with something upon her that seemed for the moment almost like cleansing.

But Penrose's London life, a curiously lonely one, after all, only lasted a very short time. Her mother was in a restless, unrooted sort of state, reluctant to take any determined step, yet unable to anchor anywhere. She had stayed on all those

years at Copsley for no particular reason,
except aversion to action, and might have
remained there in the same limpet-like
fashion if she had not been forced into
change. Now she sought about in a
vague, frightened fashion for some other
place of abode, and a sudden desire, as
strong as her nature was capable of enter-
taining, seized her to go to Cornwall, to
see the places and to breathe the air that
were once familiar to her. She would go
first to Trelewen, there was nobody there
likely to recognize her; but, in case there
might by chance be such, she would only
visit it for one day and night, then they
would take lodgings at St. Par's, the new
watering-place which had been made since
she knew it as a little fishing village,
which she had visited once or twice with
her father. She had been so drooping,
dull, and phlegmatic lately, that Penrose
and Jane were glad to see any signs of
interest or rousing in her. There was

little preparation to make and small packing. It was the end of April, a late Easter, and the weather was beautiful ; the saddest heart might pluck up hope and rejoice. Mrs. Trevenna did seem to revive under this new plan, which she was rather proud of having originated. She took a feminine pleasure in shopping before they left. She had plenty of money to spend, and had suddenly awaked to an idea that "other people" were better dressed than she and Penrose were.

"It's a shame you should be so plain, not to say shabby, Pen," she said, under the influence of this new idea. "You're as nice looking as any of these dressed-out girls. And I have hardly a decent gown either. We'll go to Regent Street, and buy some clothes."

Penrose had not been in the way of caring how she looked or what she wore, and was singularly without vanity or self-consciousness. It had never occurred to her to think if she had any good looks, though she took, perhaps, a certain pride in her long, thick, wavy brown hair; but she did not in the least know how rarely fine this was. She saw every other girl with apparent masses of hair—yellow, red, or brown, and gave them all credit for it, having no idea how much had come from a shop, and had never grown on the bedecked and beflowered heads. Still, every woman likes to have new and pretty things, and she was quite satisfied to give up an afternoon to a discursive and prolonged shopping, which was a strange joy to her mother, a pleasure she had not tasted for years. She was delighted, when the things were put on, with the vision of herself in a soft, rich silk, with a handsome mantle and bonnet, and Penrose in a pretty fawn cloth, with a hat that really suited her. It was only a regret that Penrose liked such plainly cut, quiet dresses, and would not bloom out in pinks, greens, or yellows, as her mother's taste suggested.

"You look like other girls now—like a real lady should," the mother said approvingly.

"As if she hadn't always!" Jane broke in, with indignation, as she stood by, holding a cloak on her arm, and watching with inward satisfaction. "Let her be as plain as you please, she was always a lady from top to toe; and like other girls she's *not*, but a sight better."

The words struck Penrose rather painfully. "Like other girls!" No, her heart told her this she was not—could not be. "Other girls," in the sense in which her mother spoke, had bright homes, parents who were a pride to them, a name to bear with careless, undoubting ease. Other girls had a warm place kept for them, were of much account, knew themselves admired, caressed, had no undercurrent of shame or bitterness, no inner sense of

something for ever lost and missing in
their lives.　She could never be as these
were.　But she could—she would bear
the loss, the want, the regret with un-
daunted courage ; she could make life
better for a few, and worse for no one.
She could be satisfied with less than they,
with a heart for any fate.　There was
nothing morbid about her, so she would
never know the very worst miseries of
mind.

"How different you are, Pen, from what I
was !" her mother said, half complainingly,
as Penrose turned carelessly away from
the glass, and threw off her new hat with
small concern for it.　"It was a lot to
me to be nicely dressed, and to look
pretty !"

Jane darted one swift, severe glance at
her, and pressed her long thin lips together
to keep in the words which rose in her
mind.　She only said them to herself :
"And a good thing too ; she'll not stumble

as you did through weakness or a vain mind, Mary Chegwidden."

Mrs. Trevenna went straight from London to Trelewen, her old home, which she had not seen for nearly twenty-four years. She and it were strangely altered since those days of her first bloom, when it was but a fishing-village, where a few visitors in search of boating or the picturesque straggled in summer-time. Now it had grown a crop of new terraces, neat stone houses with tiny gardens, growing nasturtiums or mignonette in front, and with its once silent stretch of sand gay and noisy with children, fathers, mothers, nurses, and loving couples. It was not the Trelewen of her memory or fancy, any more than she was pretty, rosy, smiling Molly Chegwidden. Both were gone, and she wandered, like a ghost, looking vainly for her past.. No one was left, or scarcely any one she had known, and these would not have recognized her in her heavy,

stout, pale middle age.   She was glad to
go on, and had no wish to see her birth-
place any more.   She grew more cheerful
at St. Par's, though still not the old self of
the quiet Copsley days.   The one thing
she had come to dread, in the growing
indolence and apathy which had crept
upon her by degrees, had been change;
now change was forced upon her, change
on change.   She trembled at the future,
and was confused and uneasy in the
present.   She shrank from knowing people.
If they asked questions, how should she
answer them ?   She was too slow-witted
to parry them, Penrose too absolutely
truthful.   Why, even her new name, the
name that ought to have been hers for all
these years, was difficult to pronounce,
and seemed not to belong to her.   She
often felt as if nothing belonged to her of
rights, poor soul, except her only child,
who had been hers and hers alone since
first she felt the downy head upon her

bosom. It was a strange thing that the very deed which Richard Trevenna's tardy conscience had urged him to do as her just claim, had given her no satisfaction—had only aroused the shame in her which had slept peacefully before. It was too late, as he had said, for that old wrong to be righted.

St. Par's had become of late years a much-frequented watering-place, though not a fashionable one in the ordinary use of the word. The pure delicious air, the glorious coast scenery, the firm reaches of sand, the headlands, rocks, and nooks, which made an endless variety of scene, attracted people there, even at the cost of a long tedious journey. The new grand hotel opened its hospitable—and costly—doors to the visitors, who did not mind how much they spent. There were lodging-houses of every sort and condition to suit the humbler folks.

Mrs. Trevenna had taken some very

modest rooms close to the harbour. She
was not poor ; she might, had she chosen,
have gone into handsome lodgings ; but
she had the tastes and instincts of one not
used to spending money, who rather pre-
ferred frugal ways.

Jane took her meals with them, though
at first she protested, and declared she
had rather share the landlady's kitchen.
Her sister was anxious to raise her by
degrees, without attracting notice, into the
position of her own companion ; and
Penrose hated, now that she knew the
relationship, to make any distinction
between her and them. There was
nothing vulgar, though homely, in Jane
Chegwidden, who had now taken her own
name again ; she had the innate, curious
refinement—at times proud and almost
stately—of the Cornish folk. She refused
to dress differently from her wont, though
the material of her plain dark gowns was
better, and still twisted up her fine grey

hair, as if her object was to conceal how thick it was. She looked like a quiet, superior housekeeper of the old school, and, before any stranger, kept up a dignified air of respect towards Mrs. Trevenna and Penrose which nothing would make her alter.

Penrose lost her heart to the stern, beautiful Cornish coast, which was a new revelation of Nature to her, only used to tamer scenery. The sea chafing the iron-bound shores, and for ever breaking on its weed-strewn rocks, in its glory of sapphire and emerald; the infinite variety of colour and shape, the strange carving of the age-long industry of the shifting waters; the gloom and mystery of the shadowy caves, the gleams on the sun-shiny distance—all these possessed her deepest soul. She wandered alone with her sketch-book and paint-box till she found some place where she might try, though in despair at her own futility, to catch some feeble shadow of the beauty of this new world. She could never succeed in the smallest degree to her own satisfaction, yet she was happy and absorbed, unconscious of the loneliness which was so great a contrast to the human life on the sands all about her.

She was sitting sketching one morning, rather uneasily perched on a corner of a rocky ledge, and had only looked from her painting to the sea and back again in perfect unconsciousness of the world of men and women, when she was absurdly awaked. Some one slipped on the rocks close by, fell against her, and threw her sketch-book, brushes, and box violently out of her hands at the same moment.

Penrose turned, bewildered, just in time to save the destroyer of her peace from a serious fall. She caught the slender figure of a half-laughing, half-shrieking girl, and lifted her bodily into safety.

" Oh, thank you ! How strong you are !

I am so very sorry I have disturbed you,
and made you let fall your things. Let
me try and get down and collect them
for you."

"Oh no, I can do that in a moment!"
Penrose cried earnestly. "You have hurt
yourself, I am afraid;" for the girl was
panting, in a sobbing sort of way, and
there was blood on her delicate face. She
put up her hand to feel the place on her
forehead which had been scratched, and,
seeing blood on it, she turned white and
sick in a moment, so white and faint that,
if Penrose had not held her firmly, she
would have fallen.

"It is not much," she said, eager to
console, pressing her handkerchief gently
to the cut, "only a scratch. Are you hurt
anywhere else? In pain?"

"No, no," the other said, rallying and
trying to laugh; "nowhere except just a
bruise to my foot and ankle. But I am
stupid enough to get faint at the sight of

blood." She had put her hand behind her with a shudder.

"Sit down here, on this ledge; lean back. There, now you are comfortable, and I will get my sponge wet, and just wipe the blood off your hand and forehead. I have a bit of plaster in my pocket. Are you better now?"

"Yes, thank you. You are very kind, and I have bothered and interrupted you awfully. I was sitting up above there, watching you paint, when I moved, and missed my footing somehow, and slipped. Please to pick up your things, and go on painting. I shall be perfectly right now."

"I will as soon as I have plastered up your cut; it is really nothing—it has stopped bleeding; but you look pale still."

"I soon lose all my colour—I am the most idiotic person about such things. I try to believe I can't help it, and my *mater* is always fussing about my health, so you must imagine I am delicate, and excuse me."

Penrose was looking earnestly at the girl, whose pretty face seemed a little familiar to her. She did look delicate; the soft flitting colour, the transparency of skin which showed the blue veins so clearly, the faint violet tint in the hollow round the beautiful blue eyes, gave her an appearance almost of fragility carried out by her extreme slenderness. Her little wrists, throat, and waist seemed hardly strongly made enough for any useful pur-pose. Penrose was not thick-set, though there was plenty of strength in her elastic well-knit frame, but she thought her throat and waist must be double the size of this fairy thing's. She was as frail and lovely as the pink sea-shell on the sands, as easily broken or injured. Her weak-ness, as well as her beauty, appealed to Penrose with a fascination that grew upon her. Everything was in harmony—the sweet, light, half-pathetic, half-lively voice, the wistful girlishness of her eyes, and the delicate rosy-tipped, slender white hands, from which Penrose had instantly wiped the small crimson smear which disgusted her. She could not help looking at this lovely hand, which had a sparkling ring on the taper third finger. What a contrast it made to the brown, rather large, well-formed, capable one which held it! Penrose laughed at the difference between the two.

" Your hand makes mine look browner and rougher than ever!" she said, holding one a moment beside the other. " Doesn't even sea air alter the colour a little bit ? "

" I have not been here long enough to get burnt. We only came yesterday. I wasn't very well, and our doctor ordered a mild, bracing sea air, so some one put this place into mother's head. It was

a horribly tiring long journey. I was
worn out last night, but to-day is so fine,
I am really glad we came. I wandered
away from the others, my mother and
friends—and was fascinated by this corner,
and by your sketching. Please go on
with it. I feel so ashamed of interrupting
you—you won't mind my sitting here and
looking on ? "

"Not at all," Penrose answered, collect-
ing her property, and removing what sand
she could from it. "But I cannot do
anything here worth looking at; I have
never tried sea or rocks before, and I
find them dreadfully difficult, not to say
impossible."

"Oh, but I think it is quite lovely!"

The soft caressing voice seemed almost
insincere to Penrose, though it was not so.
It was the girl's natural instinct and habit
to speak like this; she probably said more
than she felt, because she was accustomed
to do so, but intended no untruth. For

a moment this idea turned Penrose
against her; the charm was too strong
to do so altogether, yet she rather curtly
repudiated the flattery.

"It is anything but lovely. My sea is
muddy, and my rocks look like—I don't
know what—lost luggage—dry bones—
anything but rocks decked out with living
things."

"It is wonderfully good to my un-
educated eyes, at any rate," the other
returned. "I am one of those stupid
people who can't do anything. I never
could. My governesses and masters all
gave me up as hopeless. I couldn't play
the piano, so I tried the guitar, the zither,
even the banjo, and did every bit as badly
at each; I can't draw, or even do pretty
needlework. I am simply a duffer. Now
I am sure *you* are clever with your hands
as well as your head."

"No," Penrose said abruptly, and
with decision. "I can draw, to a certain

extent, and I can sew, certainly ; but I am *not* clever in any way."

"Everything is comparative. I believe I should find you so in comparison with my own stupidity. Perhaps one thing is, I've been spoilt by having things done for me."

"That is very likely," Penrose remarked absently ; she was frowning over the difficulties of her work.

The girl behind her laughed a little— it was the most musical rippling little laugh ; but Penrose vaguely wondered what amused her. There was a brief silence, broken by the looker-on.

"Have you been long here ? "

"A week only."

"And do you stay long ? "

"I can't tell yet—probably not."

"Where are you ? Not at the hotel ? "

"Oh no, at Bellevue Terrace—number three—— "

"Those little houses close to the

harbour? I noticed them because the postman said there was a Mrs. Trevenna there."

"Yes. It is my mother."

"Not really! How strange! But I suppose Trevenna must be a common Cornish name?"

"It may be," Penrose returned, a little abruptly; "but why is it strange?"

The young lady gave a little nervous laugh. If Penrose had been looking at her instead of at her drawing, she would have seen the loveliest rosy colour on her face.

"Well, I—I am very much interested in the name. Have you, by chance, any relation called Geoffrey Trevenna?"

"We have no relations, as far as I know."

"Oh! That is odd—it *is* altogether a coincidence. My name, I suppose, will be the same as yours, some day."

Penrose turned quickly, there was

surprise and confusion on her candid face.
" The same as mine ! You mean——"

" I mean that my *fiancé* is called
Geoffrey Trevenna. I dare say there is
no connection ; but it surprised me to hear
that it was your name—perhaps, because
I felt somehow as if we were friends, or
going to be friends—you were so kind to
me, you looked so kind when I bothered
you, and upset all your arrangements.
Forgive my saying that I took quite a
fancy to you. I hope we shall meet
again. I have to bathe, and none of my
people here do. I wonder whether you
will bathe with me ? "

She expected her graceful advances to
be instantly and warmly received ; she
was used to nothing but petting and
admiration, and a curious gravity and
hesitation plainly visible in the other girl
surprised and vexed her.

" I cannot promise," Penrose said,
hesitating and turning away. " My

mother—I mean we may be going away —we know no one."

"Oh, if you don't wish it — of course——"

The tone was piqued, hurt even, and Penrose was sorry, very sorry. She would not have hurt the charming, frail-looking creature for the world. She felt a pang, which was almost as sharp as one she endured as a child when she trod on a little young bird.

"It isn't that I do not wish." She spoke abruptly, the more so from the very effort to explain, from the need of being truthful, which was part of herself. "I should dearly like it; but the real fact is—I can't tell you why, but it *is* a fact—that we don't go into society. I don't belong to your world. I do assure you it is not from rudeness or unfriendliness."

They were interrupted by a prim voice below, the voice of a superior upper servant, saying, "If you please, Miss

Field, your mother thinks you have sat long enough now. The sun is in, and she hopes you will put on this wrap."

"What rubbish, Firth," Viola said sharply, the sweetness of her voice suddenly changing into that haughty brevity which certain ladies adopt with the maids who have ceased to bear Christian names in their service. "I am not in the least cold—I hate to be coddled. I shall come presently, before lunch time."

Firth retired, and Penrose wondered at a world where any one so soft could find it possible to speak to another woman with such scant courtesy. Truly it was not her world!

"I wonder what you mean," Viola went on, returning to her former sweetness in a moment, "as to being in society? If you mean of the upper ten, we are not; we are only middle-class. My father's name is Field. I am called Viola—a

ridiculously sentimental name, isn't it?
My *mater* fancied it.   What is yours?"

"Penrose."

"Penrose Trevenna!   How pretty and
uncommon!   I never heard of a woman
called Penrose—it is a surname, isn't
it?"

"I don't know."

"Well, it sounds almost like a man's
name, yet not quite.   It suits you.   I
shan't forget it, nor you.   Do you know,
you are as unlike other people as your
name is."

"Am I?   Why?"   Penrose asked
gravely.

"I don't know, I can't explain.   I am
not clever at putting things into words,
only I feel it somehow.   When I saw you,
before I made that very unceremonious
introduction of myself bodily upon you,
I thought you looked as if you had been
part of a story.   There was something
in your face different from most girls—

from any girl I had ever met. If I had been in trouble, I should have asked you for help in a moment."

"Should you ? I am very glad." The strong cordial voice was full of sincere pleasure. Penrose smiled at the girl above her. The frank sudden brightness that came like sunshine over her face, made it beautiful for the moment. "I am sure I should be ready to help you !"

"Yet you won't even bathe with me ?" Viola put on a mock pathetic voice. "You absolutely refuse to be sociable !"

"That is another thing. I know I could not be."

"You will let me come and watch you another day, if I find you painting ? "

"Oh yes, if you care to do so ; but it is dull work for you."

"No, you are not dull. I assure you I find it quite interesting. Let me see what time it is. Goodness, one already ; and there is poor *mater* frantically gesticulating. I must go up to lunch. Are you coming too ? "

" Not just yet. We have dinner at two."

" Are you a large party ? "

" No ; only three."

" Any sisters or brothers ? "

" No ; I have none."

" Nor have I, so we can sympathize ; though I can't say I ever lament the fact very bitterly. Being an only child I get all the spoiling, and I have heaps of girl friends. On the whole they do as well, I fancy, as sisters. Well, good-bye, Miss Trevenna. I am not in danger of forgetting your name. In spite of what you say, I hope we shall meet again."

She went away with a smiling, gracious little nod of half-condescending friendliness, and Penrose watched her with interest, which was almost love. She was a fascinating revelation—something new, sweet, alluring. The spoilt darling of her parents, of fortune, of love. There was no envy, not a trace, in the sense of deep unlikeness between them, which forced itself upon her. No ; envy was too small and mean a thing for her generous heart to harbour. She was glad to think that some were born into the sunshine ; she was used to the shade, it did not hurt her. She little guessed what life had in store for Viola Field, what there was to be between them some day. Meanwhile, the rapidly formed half-intimacy ended abruptly for the time. When Penrose told her mother, because she was in the habit of being outspoken, of her talk on the rocks, Mrs. Trevenna shrank with a kind of peevish terror from the idea of any further intercourse.

" Don't talk any more to her, Pen," she said, almost angrily ; "she knows a Trevenna. Who can tell that it is not a relation. I know nothing of Mr. Trevenna's people. It is much more comfortable not having to do with people now."

So Penrose, to humour her mother—she was too much in the habit of doing so to hesitate on the score of any wishes of her own—managed to go farther away for her sketching, and beyond just a hurried nod and smile, had no more intercourse with Viola during the time they remained at St. Par's.

Mrs. Trevenna wished to move again before long, and they went elsewhere, in an aimless kind of search for a resting-place, which seemed never to present itself quite as the mother hoped or vaguely wanted it to be.

CHAPTER XIII.

THE deceitful rally of health which had begun about the time of Mr. Trevenna's momentous visit to London lasted during the summer and autumn of the year. It was so marked even, that he was actually induced to go abroad, and persuaded his old friend Grey to accompany him. It is true there were intervals of pain and gloom, which made him intolerable to himself, and difficult even to so gentle a soul as Edmund Grey; but, when these were over, he seemed now and then restored to something of the uncertain brilliancy, which had made the moody, capricious, untrustworthy man at times possessed of a fitful but definite charm.

There was never any prediction to be safely made, never any security about him; in opinions, feelings, actions, he varied and shifted as a vane on a steeple on a gusty day. At times he had strong compunction for his own past ways, he was sad, quiet, gently regretful, full of noble sentiment, sincerely—for the moment —on the side of the angels. At others a blast of hatred, contempt, morose cynicism came over him, and he had no beliefs, no hopes, no affections.

Mr. Grey had a charitable, if ill-founded theory, to bring to bear on these alternations. When Dick was "himself," he was sound at heart, there was real goodness in him; when he was in his bad mood he was "not himself," that is to say, his illness, the long wearing torment of the last years of his life, had unhinged his mind, unsettled his brain, injured his heart. He never could help loving and believing in him ; he had an infinite, a most motherly sort of patience for the man who had from the first dazzled and enslaved his affections. And this tenderness of his, whether well or ill founded, was certainly calculated to bring out the better side of the contradictory, perverse, yet weak nature of the friend who knew, at the bottom of his heart, how little he had deserved it. It had prevailed at times over the worst devils of his mind, and had exorcised them for a while ; it had persuaded him into a conviction that he had done wrong to Mary Chegwidden, and, as we have seen, led to that late repentance and its fruits. Now and then it had "almost persuaded him to be a Christian." At least he was less of a heathen, less of a cynic with Grey than with all the rest of the world. Unconsciously to himself, he clung with desperate tenacity to the seemingly weaker and more yielding nature, which, for all outward seeming, had a strength which Richard Trevenna never reached. The stern, rugged mask of the one concealed the fatal weakness which had wrecked and spoilt his own life certainly, and possibly more than his own; the hesitating mildness which characterized the other externally was also a mask, for beneath there was the undeviating rectitude and principle which might have steeled the timid, shy, nervous nature into resolute endurance of a fiery ordeal for truth's sake.

In November, as the grey days shortened, and the sere leaves fell shivering from their stalks, Richard Trevenna's brief spell of ease ended with the last smile of the year. A chill, a something, perhaps only the insidious progress of his disease, prostrated him. It was the beginning of the end. As he grew rapidly weaker the pain which he had endured for years lessened, however. He did not

suffer much from anything but weariness
of body and soul, and the same subtle
change came in his every condition, the
precursor of the last change of all. He
was strangely quiet, and even gentle. His
man-servant was puzzled to account for
the absence of his usual sneers, growls,
and occasional passion of abuse ; he was
considerate and almost kind. The servants shook their heads over the singular
alteration, as an omen of the approaching
end. They did not love him, naturally,
but they had an easy place, high wages,
good living, and plenty of liberty. They
did not desire him to die. As for his one
friend, his faithful, constant companion,
this change affected him deeply, but with
a sad kind of rejoicing. Dick was "himself" now, his better self. It was something, everything to have this softened
gleam to recall before the evening deepened
to night.

One afternoon he found Mr. Trevenna,

as usual, stretched on his lounge-chair
beside the fire, with no other light than
what its red glow made, and the last
greenish light where the sunset had
been. A pale, wistful half-circle of moon
showed between the rifts of a purple grey
cloud. Only just a word of greeting
passed between them. They were too
much used to each other to be generally
talkative. Mr. Grey drew his usual chair
to the fire, and warmed first one hand,
then another with mechanical regularity.
Suddenly the harsh-toned voice, which
illness had slightly subdued, broke upon
the stillness of the room.

"I believe my brain must be softening.
I can't otherwise account for the foolish-
ness I have been thinking over to-day. I
was reading *King Lear* this morning, and
it took hold of me rather, and afterwards
I kept dwelling on that wonderful Cordelia,
on the daughterhood that he thrust away
—and I felt, like. a fool, that it might be

rather agreeable to have a daughter to be with one at times."

"And you *have* a daughter. You remembered that, Dick?" Mr. Grey cried eagerly, his whole thin, meagre body twitching and working with his sudden new idea.

"I did, perhaps; but it's a weak, sentimental, idiotic thing to think of. What's Hecuba to me, or I to Hecuba? I brought a child casually into this detestable world some twenty odd years ago, for which she owes me a grudge, and have done nothing absolutely from that time to this to make the fact anything but a curse to her. She has great reason, hasn't she, to bless her father, eh?"

"She *is* your child, for all that. Why not—why not try and see if she—if they can be any satisfaction to you? Send for them. You said you w-w-would." Mr. Grey, as usual, began to stammer in his speech, as he always did when moved, and to make strange contortions of his spare frame and feeble limbs. Mr. Trevenna was too much used to his habits now to be disturbed by them, though small, fidgety eccentricities worried and irritated him in everybody else.

" No, no, no, Edmund ; it cannot be. My case is past that gentle optimism of yours to treat. I am not fool enough to buoy myself up with the false and ridiculous hope that either of these two can ever be anything to me but strangers, if not enemies. If the girl knows all about the past and loves her mother, it is very likely she may be that also ; but I acquit poor Mary, who never had any enmity, or a drop of gall in her nature. Perhaps it did not go deep enough. I said I would send for her—and I suppose the girl must come too—when I am actually dying ; Brett and you must determine when. I am only half dying now, and I cannot face the complications, the explanations, their appearing would involve. I have grown —I suspect I always was—a coward. I do not care to tell Geoffrey yet that he is supplanted."

Mr. Grey's feelings led him to writhe and twist more painfully than ever, and when he tried to speak it was a moment or two before he was perfectly coherent.

" It—it—it isn't r-right to G-G-Geoffrey, Dick ; it isn't, indeed. He ought to know —to be p-p-prepared."

" Oh, for God's sake, Edmund, leave the thing alone ! " Trevenna cried with sudden vehemence. " To please you, or for some other equally cogent reason, I went in for the right and wrong of the affair, and satisfied your scruples or my own stupid conscience ; let that suffice. Surely I am martyrized enough already without letting myself be riddled with the arrows of per- petual annoyance. Geoffrey has chosen to neglect me, to go against my wishes, to show himself ungrateful and selfish ; he must put up with his disappointment. He's got the girl and her money to console him.   Let me be, if you have any pity for me in you ! "

"Dick ! As if—as if I had anything else ! "   The kind voice was broken as with tears ; if the room had been light perhaps his eyes might have been seen to be full too.

He stretched out his hand, and laid it hesitatingly on his friend's knee. " I would not make anything worse for you to bear, God knows, old fellow ! "

"Yes, yes, God knows, and I know, that's enough."   The angry voice sank again into the dreary gentleness which had before characterized it.   " I know it's only that there's something in you that forces you to protest for the absolute right.   But you see, old man, that's not for me ; I have been stumbling and hurting myself all along in crooked ways, and I can't

attain to doing absolutely good deeds,
only here and there I clutch at one that
seems to my purblind moral sense not entirely evil. It is certain I have not made
a very satisfactory thing out of my life.
Mine never was a successful or flowery
sort of evil doing ; the thorns of the forbidden roses, the poison of the forbidden
fruits, always remained for my share. I
made an utter mess of everything. If
instead of patching up this belated marriage,
which is nothing but a name, I had been
fool enough to take Mary Chegwidden to
live in an orthodox fashion, I should no
doubt have sickened of it and of her ; but
I shouldn't have been as I am now, alone,
but for you, without any woman's comfort-
ing. The girl might have been a daughter
indeed. But it was fate. I never did
anything good, bad, or indifferent, that
ended satisfactorily. You know what was
the thing that turned everything to bitter
—don't you ? I never told you anything

definite about Valerie Durocher—but you guessed ? "

"I know she was a bad woman—false to you, false to her husband."

"Yes. I suppose she was. But I never could judge her. I never could get her into the right perspective for that. She was the only woman I ever really loved. She turned me against poor Molly. I hoped to have married her after her divorce; but she had only been playing with me. All the same I could have forgiven that woman any crime. Molly's fault was that she bored me; she had no crimes, I exhausted her so soon. She was of the stuff to make an honest bourgeoise wife of, and somehow got into the wrong groove. I wish I had never seen her; but I've never done anything but wish in vain all my life. Well, it can't last much longer. At one time that thought made me feel a sort of terror—it doesn't now. If there's another life it can't be much worse than this one, and if not—there's falling to sleep and forgetting. I wonder what sort of an affair Mrs. Trevenna and her daughter will make of their inheritance ! Mind, she's not to be sent for till I'm *in extremis.*"

The end of the spoilt, restless, unsatisfactory life came a little before Christmas. A sudden change took place, first with convulsions, and then unconsciousness. It was in this stage that Mr. Grey wrote to Mrs. Trevenna under cover to the lawyer, who was also summoned. He felt it his duty also to write to Geoffrey ; but, though he considered that he ought to tell him of the changed condition of affairs he would find on his arrival, he could not in a letter. He deferred it till he was actually there, then he would meet him at the station and tell him. The letter, however, did not reach Geoffrey at once ; he had gone on circuit to the north, and it was redirected and sent from one place to another, so that when he arrived at Oxford his uncle had been dead two days. This information was the first Mr. Grey gave him as he met him in his most halting and confused fashion.

" Dead !" Geoffrey started back, and his dark, handsome, nonchalant face paled and showed real feeling. " And I wasn't there —poor old man !"

" It was rather sudden—not—not painful at last. Geoffrey, before we go there, I've s-s-something to tell you that you must know at once ; let us go into the waiting-room for a minute—there's no one there."

Geoffrey followed him in surprise and some alarm. He suddenly recalled Mr. Hamley's ominous warnings at Viola's birthday dance. Mr. Grey looked tragically moved ; grief alone—though it must be strong for the loss of the friend of the greater part of his life—could hardly account for his extreme agitation.

He drew a chair close up against the

one Geoffrey took, in silence, in the dull, half-lighted waiting-room, and said, almost in his ear, in a confused, stumbling whisper—

"You — you will be s-s-surprised, Geoffrey. It will be a sh-sh-shock and dis-disappointment to you. I felt you ought to have known of it before. You—you—you are not the heir to your uncle's property." The final words came out with spasmodic haste.

"I am not! Do you mean to say my uncle has left it away from me? Was he so angry as all that? Well, he is dead. He *was* kind to me—once. I will try not to resent it. He had a right—— "

"Stop. Hush, Geoffrey. Wait till you understand. Whether his being vexed with you or not had anything to do with it I—I am not p-p-prepared to say. It is not the main issue. There are others —nearer to him—who have a closer claim."

"Others! What can you mean? I never heard of any one."

"No. But it is true, for all that, that they exist. Your uncle's *wife* was with him at the last."

"*My uncle's wife?*"

"Yes. He was married, though they did not live together."

"And he kept that fact secret—from me—for how long?"

"Not for long. Geoffrey, I cannot have you deceived. I trust to your generosity, to your gentlemanly feelings to keep others from knowing what I tell you now. Your uncle only married this—this poor lady last spring. He felt, very late in the day, that he owed it to her."

"But you spoke of more than one," Geoffrey said, quietly and coldly. He was capable of much self-control, and the habits of his class kept him from showing either anger or disgust, but he was aware that the foundations of many an air-castle were falling in ruin about him as his old friend unwove the riddle of his uncle's past.

"Yes. I—I—in fact, there is a—a—a daughter."

"Then I am the richer by an aunt and cousin ! It is certainly a surprise— a very great, not exactly an agreeable, surprise. I shall find this—this poor lady, as you call her—and her daughter at Redwood ? "

"Yes. You will, I know, make as little disagreeableness as you can. Believe me, Geoffrey," the little man went on, forgetting to stammer in the earnestness of his sympathy, " I have had nothing to do with keeping you in the dark. I urged my poor friend to tell you. He shrank from it. I—I loved him, Geoffrey, you know that. We were friends, unbroken friends for nearly forty years, yet I cannot deny that he did wrong. He had a want

of moral courage ; but his constant sufferings—bodily and mental sufferings—must
be taken into account.   No one but I
knew what those sufferings were.   They
—they amounted to anguish.   You can
forgive much to one who has had so much
to bear, Geoffrey, cannot you ? "

" I will try and remember the times
when he was good to me," Geoffrey said,
not untouched by the intensity of the
appeal in the sad voice that pleaded for
the man who was gone out of the pain of
life into the silence of non-existence, whom
neither hate nor gratitude now could
reach.

"And the position of—of Mrs. Trevenna
is a peculiar, a painful one, you will remember that ?   But I need not ask you ;
I am *sure* you will spare her as much as
you can."

" It is not my way to be rough on
women, whatever they are.   You will
forgive my feeling that Mrs. Trevenna

cannot, from the nature of that position you speak of, be a very estimable
person."

" She did wrong once," Mr. Grey
returned, with more force and decision
than Geoffrey had expected. " There are
not many of us who have not this to avow.
With that one exception I believe her to
be a good woman. She was much more
sinned against than sinning. Come, shall
we be going ? "

Geoffrey rose in silence. He did not
attempt any answer to the last statement.
Inwardly he felt cynically sceptical of
Mrs. Trevenna's worth. It was just like
good old Quixotic Grey to champion
her. What did he know of women ?
Little enough of the best specimens,
absolutely nothing of the baser sort. At
any rate, whatever she was, adventuress
or not, virtuous or vile, the case was not
altered. He was ousted—he had been
shamefully deceived. He was too much

of a gentleman as well as man of the
world to make a scene, to pose as a victim ;
but his mind was naturally not disposed
to admit a favourable idea of the persons
who had deposed him. He must go through
with all the unpleasantness before him
with as much appearance of indifference
as "good form" insisted upon. He was
not going to behave like a cad, however
ill he had been treated ; but as to taking
old Grey's opinion on such a subject—
he mentally shrugged his shoulders, and
prepared, with outward good breeding and
inward disgust, to go through the trials
that awaited him. He dared not speculate
much on the future ; the present had to
be met, if not with patience, at least with
well-bred stoicism. He wasn't going to
show these women, this new-found wife
and daughter, that he cared, that they,
in their promotion, had to tread upon
his hopes. He wouldn't give them a
chance of triumphing over his disappoint-

ment. He would at least overawe them into respect. He did not mean to wear his heart on his sleeve for such very common daws to peck at.

END OF VOL. I.

PRINTED BY WILLIAM CLOWES AND SONS, LIMITED,
LONDON AND BECCLES.   *G., C. & Co.*

www.ingramcontent.com/pod-product-compliance
Lightning Source LLC
Chambersburg PA
CBHW020848020726
47497CB00005B/1307